PRAISE FOR
American as Paneer Pie

A JUNIOR LIBRARY GUILD SELECTION

"Addresses important issues of racism, colorism, and xenophobia through a well-drawn narrator whose political evolution is fascinating to watch."—*Kirkus Reviews*

"A tender depiction of a young girl navigating prejudice and finding ways to be her whole self in the process."
—*School Library Journal*

"Kelkar illuminates the need for voices raised against discrimination and paints a convincing portrait of a girl straddling two cultures."—*Publishers Weekly*

"Succeeds valiantly at exposing the conflicted loyalties felt by many children of immigrants."—*Shelf Awareness*

"A story that desi outcasts throughout the country can empathize with."—*Booklist*

SIMON & SCHUSTER
BOOKS FOR YOUNG READERS

NEW YORK
LONDON
TORONTO
SYDNEY
NEW DELHI

American as PANEER PIE

Supriya Kelkar

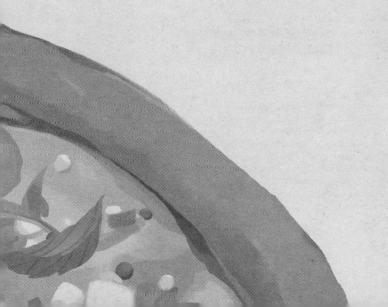

SIMON & SCHUSTER BOOKS FOR YOUNG READERS
An imprint of Simon & Schuster Children's Publishing Division
1230 Avenue of the Americas, New York, New York 10020

This book is a work of fiction. Any references to historical events, real people, or real places are used fictitiously. Other names, characters, places, and events are products of the author's imagination, and any resemblance to actual events or places or persons, living or dead, is entirely coincidental.

Text © 2020 by Supriya Kelkar

Cover illustration © 2020 by Abigail Dela Cruz

Cover design by Laura Lyn DiSiena © 2020 by Simon & Schuster, Inc.

All rights reserved, including the right of reproduction in whole or in part in any form.

SIMON & SCHUSTER BOOKS FOR YOUNG READERS and related marks are trademarks of Simon & Schuster, Inc.

For information about special discounts for bulk purchases, please contact Simon & Schuster Special Sales at 1-866-506-1949 or business@simonandschuster.com.

The Simon & Schuster Speakers Bureau can bring authors to your live event. For more information or to book an event, contact the Simon & Schuster Speakers Bureau at 1-866-248-3049 or visit our website at www.simonspeakers.com.

Also available in an Aladdin hardcover edition

Interior design by Laura Lyn Disiena

The text for this book was set in Century Expanded

Manufactured in the United States of America

0123 OFF

First Simon & Schuster Books for Young Readers paperback edition May 2021

10 9 8 7 6 5

The Library of Congress has cataloged the hardcover edition as follows:

Name: Kelkar, Supriya, 1980- author.

Title: American as paneer pie / Supriya Kelkar

Description: First edition. | New York : Aladdin, [2020] | Audience: Ages 8-12. | Audience: Grades 3-7. | Summary: When a racist incident rocks her small Michigan town, eleven-year-old Lekha must decide whether to speak up or stay silent, even as she struggles to navigate her life at home, where she can be herself, and at school, where she is teased about her culture.

Identifiers: LCCN 2019015822 (print) | ISBN 9781534439382 (hardcover) | ISBN 9781534439399 (paperback) | ISBN 9781534439405 (eBook)

Subjects: Immigrants—Fiction | East Indian Americans—Fiction | Prejudices—Fiction | Bullying—Fiction. | Self confidence—Fiction | Hate crimes—Fiction | Middle schools—Fiction | Schools—Fiction

Classification: PZ7.1.K417 Am 2020 (print) | LCC PZ7.C179 (eBook) | DDC [Fic]

LC record available at https://lccn.loc.gov/2019015822

To Arjun, Leykh, and Zuey,
my everything, from A to Z

chapter ONE

*I*t's funny how something as small as a dot could matter so much.

But it did.

Most Desi kids I knew had been asked about it at some point in their lives. "Do you have a dot?" "Where's your dot?" "Why do you guys have dots on your forehead?" It was kind of annoying.

But I didn't know any Desi kids who had to walk around with a bindi on their forehead at all times. I had to, though. For eleven years and counting. That's because mine was a birthmark. A bindi-size, dark-brown freckle that I couldn't take off. And that was *really* annoying.

But despite how much I wanted to forget my permanent

bindi at school, I loved looking at the real bindis I had at home. And on this Friday night, I was staring at the mother lode. Ignoring the cobwebs draped around my dimly lit basement, I sifted through white packets full of bindis of every color and size. There were neon circles; jewel-tone diamonds; pastel, snakelike swirls; and metallic, oblong spears.

While I loved staring at the glimmering bindis, they weren't what I was looking for. I broke free of their hypnotic spell and peered into the box full of knickknacks from India. There were glittery bangles, shimmering decorative cloth with hundreds of tiny mirrors sewn into the embroidered cotton, and sparkling gold and red coasters. We clearly liked shiny things. It was the Desi way.

I paused at my permanent bindi's reflection in the mirrors of a soft blue pillowcase. I quickly adjusted the long diagonal sweep of thick black curls I kept pinned over the birthmark, and then I spotted what I had been searching for. Four dandiya. And, yes, they were sparkly too.

I grabbed the wooden sticks that had been wrapped in green and orange fabric with ribbons of gold spinning around them and shut the box. It was just in time, as thundering footsteps made their way down the stairs, getting louder and louder. You'd think it was a giant coming in search of whoever's beanstalk had invaded his yard. But it was just my next-door neighbor Noah. He was as scrawny as me, but somehow his footsteps made him seem stronger.

I had shown Noah a video from my cousin's wedding during our last trip to India almost three years ago. Our side is Marathi, and the bride's side is Gujarati. All five hundred guests did raas together, the Gujarati folk dance with sticks that seems more like a fun game than a dance. Despite my great-uncle's grumbling about the noise, we had a blast, jumping, twirling, and hitting sticks to the beat of the catchy music.

Apparently, it showed, because as soon as Noah saw that video, he asked me to teach him. And since then, every year around Navratri, the Hindu holiday celebrated with nine nights of raas at the Hindu temples in Detroit, Noah would play raas here.

We lived an hour away from Metro Detroit, and were the only Indian family in town, so it was nice to be able to have someone to play raas with, even if that someone had a hard time pronouncing the word and we were doing it a couple of weeks late.

"Just in time," I said, turning with the dandiya.

Noah was wearing a lumpy, crocheted gray fish hat with uneven, oddly shaped eyes that bugged out.

I laughed so hard, I almost dropped the dandiya. "What is *that*?"

Noah shrugged, grinning. "My dad's latest creation."

"A whale?" I guessed, looking at the wide face of the frumpy, half-collapsed hat.

"A whale? Uncool, Lekha," said Noah, pretending to be offended. "It's a shark. And a dolphin. A sharkphin, actually. It's a dolphin for tomorrow morning, to wish you luck at tryouts."

"Thanks," I said, nervous butterflies fluttering. I tried to remain calm about the swim team tryouts where I might finally become a full-fledged member of the Dolphins.

"Except I'm not going to wear it there . . . cuz, you know . . . it looks like this. And I don't want to embarrass you on your big day. But tomorrow night, on Halloween, I will be wearing it. Because on Halloween, it's going to be the shark to your Michael Phelps."

This time I did drop the dandiya. They rolled on the thin brown Berber carpet. "Really?"

Noah nodded.

Every year we flipped a coin to see who got to pick the costumes. For the past two Halloweens, ever since he wanted to be a reporter, Noah had won, and we went as some random newspaper reference I didn't get (but the grown-ups who answered the doors strangely found adorable). I was bummed when Noah won again this year. I'd wanted to go as Michael Phelps and a shark ever since Dad showed me an old online video of the Olympic swimmer racing a computer-animated shark. "We're really not going as those reporters?"

"No Woodward and Bernstein. I realized it wasn't really fair for me to pick our costumes three Halloweens in a row. So here I am, the shark from your little video, even though no one is going to get it. I swear, your costume ideas are even more out-there than mine."

I shrugged, grateful I wouldn't be in Dad's old suit tomorrow. "*Whale*, I guess they are."

"No. We're not doing this," said Noah, picking up his pair of dandiya.

"Oh, I *sea*," I said, grabbing my sticks. After we learned about puns in fourth grade, I started to make them every now and then to annoy Noah, who thought newspaper articles were art and puns were the pits. "You don't want me to make puns on *porpoise*."

"You're *shrimp*ossible," Noah replied, trying not to smile.

"That's a good one." I beamed. "I need to remember that for next time."

"Just play the music, please." Noah handed me his cell phone. My parents didn't let me have one because Dad thought I was too young and Aai thought it was too much radiation. Noah threw one of his dandiya in the air and caught it. "I could do a piece on raas for the *Gazette*," he said, his "raas" sounding more like "Ross."

The thought of everyone at school reading about this made my palms sweaty. "Trust me. No one is interested in an Indian dance." I wished Noah would drop it. That he would understand, without me having to explain, that I didn't need another reason for people to ask me more dot-related questions. Sometimes Noah just didn't get that highlighting how different my culture was from everyone else's at school just made everyone think I was, well, different. I scrolled down Noah's browser and got a garba-raas playlist up. "Ready?" I asked, twirling one of my dandiya like a baton as the music started to speed up.

Noah nodded, and I began to count.

"One." We each hit our own dandiya together, down by our knees.

"Two." We tilted our pair of sticks to the right, clinking the other's pair to form an X.

"Three." We tilted to the left and made another X.

"Four." We tapped our own dandiya together, back down by our knees.

"Five." We took the dandiya in our right hands, hit them to each other's, and spun around until we faced each other again.

And then it was time to do it again, and again, and again, until I no longer had to count. We were just jumping and turning and almost accidentally smacking each other's fingers while cracking up. As the music grew louder, I spun fast, and my frizzy curls decided to spin too.

I stopped to slide them back over my birthmark and bobby pin them in place.

Noah, midturn, ready to hit my sticks, stopped just before he accidentally hit me instead. "Lekha!"

"What?" I asked, even though I knew what was coming next.

"You know it's fine, right? That no one cares?" he added, pointing to my forehead.

"Let's get some water," I said, changing the subject.

Noah followed me up the stairs, his footsteps booming as we passed the canvas prints of pictures my dad had taken in India. It was easy for Noah to say no one cared. But it was also untrue. Lots of people cared. If they didn't, I wouldn't have gotten made fun of for my bindi birthmark when I first started elementary school in Oakridge.

"You always do that," said Noah as I reached around an array of spiky aloe plants in the kitchen to get to the water pitcher and pour him a glass.

"Do what?"

"Change the subject when you don't want to talk about things. It's really obvious."

I gulped my water down. Before I could think of another topic to discuss, to throw this nosy reporter off the scent, a loud honking interrupted.

Noah and I looked at each other. "New neighbors?" we both said at the same time.

The dentist across the street from us had moved away from the Michigan winters, retiring on her cavity money to

Florida, making all the other old, cold people on our street jealous. We ran down the hall, skidding on the oak floor, threw on our shoes, and raced out the door. We stopped at the porch, under a swinging plastic ghost, but there was no car in the dentist's former driveway.

All we saw were my parents, raking leaves and trimming plants for winter. Dad smiled at us, his mustache scrunching up on his face. Aai gave a small wave and tossed her silky black hair back out of her eyes. I was watching her hack at the dead sticks on the rose mallow with shears when another honk startled me. It was coming from a car to our right, in Mr. Giordano's driveway.

Mr. Giordano was bent over a sign in his yard, struggling to get its metal feet into the hardening soil. Satisfied, he got into the car, and the driver pulled out of the driveway.

I could finally see the sign, but it wasn't too exciting. It just said WINTERS FOR CONGRESS.

"Ugh," said Noah. "Can you believe that?"

"Believe what?"

"He's voting for Winters. My dad says she hates anyone who looks different from her."

My smile disappeared slightly as I felt my heavy black

bun with my brown fingers. I knew I didn't look like Abigail Winters, with her blue eyes, light-brown hair, and skin the color of peeled almonds. I turned away from the sign, glancing at Noah, who was frowning and shaking his head. I could tell he was getting worked up and needed calming down. "Could you be more *Pacific*?" I asked.

"Yeah. For starters, I read in the paper that she—wait. Was that another pun?"

I grabbed Noah's sharkphin hat. "You *otter* run if you ever wanna see this again!" I raced to our backyard, my laughter echoing down the street as Noah chased after me, grinning, leaving Abigail Winters far behind.

Maybe Noah was right. Maybe I did change the subject a lot. But it was just a silly little yard sign, and he was getting so upset over it. Something that small couldn't really matter that much. Could it?

chapter TWO

The next afternoon I stared at my reflection in the Oak-ridge Sports Club locker room mirror, pulling at my swim cap like it was pizza dough. Whoever invented the swim cap must never have grown her hair down to her waist. I stretched the rubbery cap into a hungry mouth, letting it swallow the large frizzy bun that nestled my black curls together. I yanked the front of the cap down toward my eyebrows. Bye-bye, bindi birthmark. My head felt like one of those overripe green grapes Noah and I always tried to squeeze out of their skin at lunch.

A locker behind me slammed shut with a metallic clang. I didn't have to turn to know who it was. In a split second, happy, normal Home Lekha disappeared, and even though we were nowhere near the middle school, School Lekha appeared. I felt my shoulders slump, and I took a step to the side, cleansing the mirror of my reflection as Harper neared. We were both eleven, but she was a whole head taller than me. Her short thin wisps of shiny red hair hugged her earlobes as she easily snapped a swim cap on.

I felt her green eyes on the misshapen lumps in my cap. "Ready for tryouts, Leh-kuh?"

I wanted to correct her. I wished my mouth would just open and say, *"It's Lekha. LAY-khaa. You've known me since fourth grade, but you still can't say my name right."* But School Lekha only thought about what she wanted to say and never said it out loud. So I just nodded.

"Good luck. See you in the pool."

"You too," I said softly, following Harper out the locker room door, my toes clenching at the thousands of little white tiles that made up the flooring around the pool. They were wet and cold, not exactly the feelings of comfort, but they were home to me. I inhaled deeply, taking in a whiff of the chlorine fumes of the Sports Club pool.

Harper was talking to the cluster of boys splashing in the water in front of the bleachers where all the parents sat.

From his seat there, Dad was staring at his phone when Aai spotted me and nudged him. He quickly tucked his phone into his bag and got up to give me a hug.

Aai patted my head. "Think positive and do your best, okay, Lekha? If you make it or don't, it doesn't matter, as long as you give it your all."

Dad knelt down before me, silver strands of hair peeking out of his mustache. "Himmat karke," he said, telling me to be brave.

"Badha kadam," I responded softly. It meant "take that step forward." It was part of a Hindi phrase Dad had learned in medical school that meant "we're in this together." Dad had first said it to Aai when they got married and left their families in Mumbai to move to America. Aai said it gave her strength. It seemed to do the opposite for me.

"I can't hear you," said Dad.

"Badha kadam," I said a little louder.

A few of the boys in the pool began to snicker.

My cap was over my ears, but I could still hear it loud and clear. I didn't have to turn to know what they were laughing at. They were laughing at my parents. At us. People always did around here, even if it wasn't out loud or even with their mouths. The exasperated breath that huffed into the phone when the bank teller couldn't understand the questions Dad was asking, even though he was speaking in English. The rolling of eyes from the cashier at the grocery store when Aai held up the line, scanning her receipt to make sure all the coupons had been tallied up correctly. The finger-to-the-forehead gesture the fifth-grade boys made when I first started elementary school. They were all different ways of laughing at us. It was like no matter where I went or what I did, the laughter always figured out some way of finding me.

I glanced at the boys out of the side of my eyes as I headed toward the start of the lanes.

"She needs a lawn mower," giggled Liam, a short brunette boy from my English class. He made an engine noise with his lips.

"You're terrible, Liam," said Harper.

The other boys laughed even louder than before, filling the room with the sound of hollow splashes and my embarrassment.

I frowned, passing the bleachers, unsure of what Liam meant. Was he talking about our yard? Aai had banned herbicides and pesticides from our grass years ago, so it was full of weeds. Or was it about my hair? I patted the lumps in my cap, wishing I could be my normal, funny, sometimes punny self in front of Harper, or Liam, or anyone from school. But it seemed like the only person who knew both sides of me was Noah, who was standing poolside, taking a million pictures of me with a bright flash.

"Noah," I groaned, rubbing my eyes until the spots dancing in front of me disappeared. "This better not make it into the *Gazette*."

Noah sometimes hung out here when I swam, while his parents played racquetball on the other side of the club. "You didn't say 'off the record.' That means I can use it. It's for my 'Hidden Talents of the Sixth-Grade Class' piece. So far it's Emma and you."

I chewed on my lower lip. An article about me swimming was better than one about raas, but I didn't want to be in any piece, let alone one that was also about Emma. Her hidden talent was not so hidden. She painted pictures of bird droppings. I tried to focus Noah's investigational skills on something else.

"Any scoop on the new neighbors?" I flapped my arms back and forth, loosening up. We had seen the moving truck arrive this morning, but we had yet to find out who the belongings belonged to. And, more importantly, if there were any kids our age.

"Negative." Noah fiddled with his camera. "Still just a bunch of boxes with no people."

Although I wouldn't admit it to Noah, I was secretly hoping it would be a girl. I wanted to have sleepovers like Harper and her friends, and Noah just wasn't interested. He only wanted to sleep in his own bed with no one else in the room. He didn't even let his shih tzu, Cookie, snuggle up to his feet at bedtime because the one time she did, his feet fell asleep before he did.

Coach Turner whistled, motioning for all the swimmers to take their places. "Let's go! Remember, top two girls and the top boy make the team. The rest of you, I wish I had more openings, but there's always next year."

I stretched my neck up and down. I had tried out last year when there was a spot open but didn't make it. And in a year I'd be twelve. I had to do this, and I had to do it now.

"Do a really cool dive and maybe I'll get the front page." Noah gave me a fist bump. "Don't look so nervous. You've got this. Pretend the sharkphin hat is here, cheering you on," he added, heading back to his spot as Coach Turner called the swimmers to their places.

I snapped my goggles on, letting the whole room turn a shade of cool aquamarine, and walked toward Harper, reminding myself that swimming timed laps in the hundred-yard IM was something I had done so many times, I could do it as naturally as I could walk.

Harper stared straight at the water as I took my place next to her, on my starting block. Liam and the other kids took the rest of the lanes.

"Swimmers ready?" Coach asked.

His whistle blew sharply before we could even nod. But I was ready. I jumped in, letting the cold water welcome me. My legs became spaghetti as I dolphin kicked underwater. I stared down at my lane line in a swirl of blue. One . . . two . . . three . . . and inhale. I drew in a heap of oxygen and was off, churning my arms in the butterfly until I tapped the far end of the pool.

A quick turn and it was time for the backstroke. The pool was full of splashing water. I didn't know if it was from Harper or from me, and I didn't want to look to find out. Not until the last lap.

One more turn and tap on the pool wall. It was breaststroke time. My biceps burned as my arms went forward, sideways, and down, faster and faster, until I tapped the edge of the pool.

This was it. Freestyle. I turned my head from side to side, arms whipping the blue. It was time to look. I glanced to the side. Harper was right in front of me with a good lead, thanks to her backstroke and breaststroke. I ignored the pain in my legs and zipped forward, my hand in line with hers, seen briefly through the foam. I sliced into the water, faster, almost dissolving into the splashes until I finally tapped the edge.

I pulled my goggles off and glanced at the scoreboard. My name was in the middle of the alphabetically arranged kids. Lekha Divekar: 1:09.30. My fastest time ever.

"We tied!" exclaimed Harper from my left.

I scanned the scoreboard. Harper Walbourne: 1:09.30. She was right. We *had* tied. Although it may not have seemed like it in school, the way kids flocked to Harper but avoided me, she and I were equals. We had both made the swim team.

I grinned at my parents, who were clapping in the stands as Noah took picture after picture, and then turned to watch

Liam finally tap the edge. He was five seconds slower than me. I watched as he stared at the scoreboard and saw his numbers. And as awful as it was, as horrible as it made both versions of me sound, I couldn't help but feel a little good inside when the smile was wiped off his face.

Because for once, it meant no one was laughing.

chapter
THREE

*B*ack home from my triumphant swim, now as a member of the Dolphins, I listened to a song from the old Hindi movie *Dangal* on repeat as I got dressed for Halloween. The singers roared about believing in yourself and ignoring what others say, because your day will come. I bopped my head along, zipping up an old warm-up suit and squeezing a dry, too-tight swim cap on. I twirled to hit the stairwell lights and danced down, unbothered by the whistles of the pressure cooker that were shouting over my song.

"When will *Dangal* stop repeating?" asked Aai, before dropping a stack of papers on the kitchen table at the end of our small hall. She preferred soft, classical sitar music over blaring Bollywood hits.

"When I'm done celebrating," I replied, flexing my muscles.

She smiled, putting down the paperwork Coach had given her after tryouts, and headed to the stove. "Your costume looks great. You're going to have so much fun tonight."

"Thanks," I said. "Just don't follow us too closely, please?" Aai used to let me walk to elementary school with Noah because it was at the other end of our neighborhood. She didn't mind me walking down the street to the post office. But she drew the line at Halloween. Trick-or-treating started at 6:00 p.m., and by the end of October, it was already dark then.

Aai nodded, opening the pressure cooker. The nutty aroma of the cooked lentils and the fragrant basmati rice drifted through the house. "You'll have to make sure your homework is done on time the days you have swim practice. And every third Saturday of the month is a swim meet. Meets start in December for the new kids."

"I always finish my homework on time, don't I?" I barely talked back to my parents, respected my elders, got all As, didn't lie, and didn't get into trouble at school. I had checked all the boxes on the good-Desi-kid list, I thought as I danced back toward the stairs and entered the den.

I was greeted by the rich smell of the curry leaf plant growing in one of the many pots in the room that made up Dad's Jungle. Dad was crouched on the floor, gently scooping up some ants that had made their way in for the winter with a cardstock flyer from the mail for Juan Sharpe, the guy running against Winters.

"Lights, Lekha," he said, concentrating on the bugs.

I reached my hand back out through the door frame and hit the switch, turning off the lights above the stairs behind me, which I had accidentally left on. I knew what was coming next.

"What do you think it is? Diwali?" Dad grinned.

"Hilarious," I said. After the four-hundredth time hearing his joke about the festival of lights when you purposely turn on every light in the house, it was hard to fake-laugh. I stepped back into the Jungle. The citrusy scent of lemongrass wafted by from one pot, immediately followed by the floral perfume of the tiny white jasmine flowers nearby. I rounded the shelves that housed the plants and turned the music down on the computer in the crowded den.

Dad handed me the dustpan he had dropped the ants

into. "You're not too famous to show these ants out, are you, Michael Phelps?"

I grinned and shook my head, walking past more canvas prints of pictures Dad had taken in India. There was the Sikh Golden Temple, an intricately carved Jain temple, and the Hindu temple my mom had grown up going to.

"And I'll get the camera. Almost time for pictures."

I headed out to drop the ants in the front yard. I glanced at the dentist's house. The towers of moving boxes were now gone, but no new neighbors were in sight. I shivered as a fall breeze coiled around me, making the ghost dangling from our porch roof dance. It wasn't too cold yet for the little black ants, though. They were still crawling around on the plastic pan, not curling into little frozen balls like they did in winter.

To my right, Mr. Giordano was on a ladder, cleaning leaves out of the gutter. I saw him raise his eyebrows as I emptied the dustpan in the grass. He probably thought I was tossing trash there. I wanted to explain that we were vegetarian and didn't kill bugs, so instead, we caught them and put them outside. But I thought his eyebrows might fall off his forehead if he heard that.

To my left, Noah in his sharkphin hat, trick-or-treat bag

in hand, was heading over to my house with his parents. They were armed with a ton of cameras, cell phones, and camcorders. My parents joined us, and Aai handed me a pumpkin-shaped cloth bag as Noah and I took our places in front of the garage door.

We knew the routine well. Dad took his photography seriously and loved the way the last rays of light hit the garage door in the evening.

"Oh, you two!" Noah's mom beamed as we smiled for picture after picture. "Don't ever let the world take those smiles off your faces," she added, blinking back tears as she crossed her arms over her shirt, which was printed with the union logo I recognized from when Aai worked as an engineer at the transmission plant.

I scrunched my nose at Noah as the sun dipped below the horizon. He just shrugged. Clearly, he got his love of dramatic writing from his dramatic mother.

Before Mrs. Wade could burst into tears, the storm sirens went off across town. Only, they weren't to warn us about a storm tonight. They were signaling the start of trick-or-treating hours.

"It's time!" I shrieked, like I was already sugared up.

"You kids have fun," said Dad as Noah and I ran down the driveway.

First up on our route was Mr. Giordano, but he always gave out pennies in between grumbling to us about the weather, so we decided to skip him. Besides, he was busy cleaning the gutter still and seemed to have no interest in giving us anything other than dirty looks.

I glanced back at our house. My mom-bodyguard was standing at the bottom of our driveway, waiting to follow us. Maybe she would actually give us a couple of houses' distance this time, since we were eleven.

Noah and I ran up to the next neighbor's house. They had turned their entire front yard into a graveyard, with robotic skeleton hands waving in the ground and their family names on all the tombstones.

I imagined how Aai would click her tongue in disapproval at the neighbors putting their actual names on the tombstones. My mother was insistent that words had power, and you shouldn't put bad thoughts out into the world because they would come true.

Since we were two of the few kids on the street still into trick-or-treating, the neighbors loaded our bags with candy.

But about half had gelatin in it. I sighed. Gelatin meant animal parts. Animal parts meant I couldn't eat them. I'd have to give all those colorful, chewy candies to Noah.

We ran house to house, my legs feeling numb from either the cold weather or the fact that I had swum my best time earlier that day.

"Did you notice the boxes are gone?" huffed Noah as the cold air made it a little harder for him to breathe, even with his pink puffer jacket on.

I slowed down, keeping pace with Noah for the next house. "Yeah." I nodded. "But I bet they don't have kids."

"My sources say it's a girl," said Noah, knocking on the next door. "Our age."

I gasped, and it wasn't just from the gigantic candy bars this house was handing out. Our new neighbors had a girl! And she was our age! I was finally going to have a friend for sleepovers, right across the street.

Most Desi kids I knew in Detroit had jam-packed weekends, full of Bharat Natyam classes, Bollywood dance classes, classical Indian singing lessons, and nonstop social events, with dozens of holiday celebrations, temple outings, Bollywood concerts, classical music concerts, and Marathi plays added to the mix. They probably barely had time for sleepovers. But we were nowhere near Detroit. And there were zero Indian people here, so zero social events and plenty of time for sleepovers. Just no friends interested in them. But now, with our new neighbor, there was finally hope.

"Are you sure it's a girl?"

"My dad said he saw a girl carrying a box."

"Why isn't she out trick-or-treating?"

"Maybe they don't know about Halloween."

"Who doesn't know about Halloween?" I wiped at my nose as the cold air chilled it.

Noah shrugged. "Or maybe they don't believe in it. Or maybe they couldn't find the box with their costumes in it on time. Or maybe—"

"Or maybe they just don't have kids," I said again, my arms now sore from lugging my bag full of candy. I didn't need to get my hopes up unnecessarily. Even if the new neighbor was a girl our age, chances are she'd be more like Harper than like me.

Noah looked at me. "Let's find out."

"What?" I asked, shivering. My swim cap was clearly not cut out for Michigan in fall. "I'm tired. Let's just go home and stuff our faces with candy before dinner."

"Let's ring the bell. It's Halloween. And with the dentist gone, we know they won't be handing out little toothpastes. So we might get something good. Besides, we've done almost every house on the street. Let's just finish this one and then go home."

"If they can't trick-or-treat because their costumes are still boxed up, what makes you think they have candy?"

"Come on," said Noah, tugging at my arm as he turned up the new neighbors' driveway.

"Lekha!" Aai shouted from behind us. "They've just moved here. Give them some time to unpack!"

I cringed. Aai didn't have much of an accent, but she did have one. And screaming down the street with it in public was embarrassing even if no one else was around to hear it but Noah.

Noah stopped. "Their porch lights are off. Their hallway lights are off. Maybe your mom's right."

Aai was not right. I was eleven. I didn't need a chaperone to trick-or-treat on our own street. I needed some space. It was now my turn to grab Noah's arm. "Hurry up before my mom catches up."

Ignoring Aai's shouts, which were now growing louder as she speed walked toward us, we bounded up the driveway. I punched the doorbell with my finger as Noah knocked loudly on the glass and we both shouted, "Trick-or-treat!"

The door abruptly opened. And so did my mouth. Because the person who answered the door, without a costume on, was a girl our age. But she wasn't just a girl our age. She had silky black, shoulder-length hair. Her skin was brown. She was Desi.

I couldn't believe it. Another Desi family in our tiny little town! There would finally be someone to get it. To know what it's like to feel different but want to be the same as everyone else. To love your Hindi movie star posters all over your bedroom wall but to be mortified when a teacher asks you to say a word in Hindi. To know how it feels to be asked once a week where your dot is, or if you shower, or if your parents can speak English. To know what it's like to have two lives, your Indian life at home and your American life at school.

I smiled bigger than I had all day, even after making the Dolphins. "Hi! I'm Lekha, and this is Noah."

The girl smiled. "My name is Avantika. It's so great to meet you."

My smile curled slightly down at her words, and it wasn't because I could hear Aai's footsteps getting closer. It was because I was wrong. My new neighbor wasn't exactly like me, and she probably didn't know what it was like to feel everything I did. My new neighbor had a thick Indian accent. My new neighbor was a fob.

chapter

FOUR

I'm a fob too," said Dad from behind the kitchen counter as he squeezed a cheesecloth until a light-yellow liquid came out of what was wadded inside. "Fresh off the boat."

I was eating my Halloween candy out of the bag, but my thoughts were on what Dad was making. As he unwrapped the cloth, revealing the clumpy white paneer inside, I chewed faster. It was partly because I didn't know if my parents were going to make me hand over what little candy I had left after the great gelatin purge to make Avantika feel welcome here. And it was partly because I was starving; the Indian cheese was one of my favorites, and Dad made it really well.

"You are not a fob," I replied, watching as he formed the cheese into little cubes in preparation for the big dinner he and Aai had planned for our new neighbors. "Your accent isn't that thick. You came here a long time ago. You know how things work around here."

Dad made a disapproving clicking noise with his tongue.

"I feel so bad for anyone who has just come from India. You kids act as if you're better than them," said Aai from the kitchen table. She was chopping up tomatoes and garlic, adding them to a bowl with some mint leaves from the Jungle.

"She's right," said Dad, heating up some oil in a cast-iron pan. "You guys just laugh at the accents of anyone from India, thinking how funny it is to hear someone say a word differently than you do. But what you should be thinking is, 'Wow, that person can communicate in at least two languages.' Something you can't do, can you? Or should we ask your aaji?"

I cringed, thinking of my conversations with my grandmother in India. I used to speak Marathi when I was a little kid, but I quickly gave it up once I started elementary school at Oakridge. Even though I still understood Marathi, I could barely speak it now. My accent was so thick, I could barely say the *r* right, and everything sounded funny. So, every weekend during our calls to India, I'm forced to have the same conversation with Aaji. "How are you?" "I'm fine. How are you?" "I'm fine. How are—" and then I hand the phone over to Dad, my ears burning red from embarrassment.

"Do you have any idea how hurtful it must feel to people new to this country to be made fun of just for being Indian? You're lucky you didn't ever experience that."

I stopped shoving chocolate in my mouth, suddenly feeling more annoyed than hungry. If only Dad knew just how often I got made fun of just for being Indian.

"And by a fellow Desi, too," said Aai, bringing the tomatoes and garlic to the pan and tossing them in. "If you call them fobs, they can call you ABCDs and you can't complain."

"Nobody says that," I retorted over the crackling of the oil.

"Sure they do. 'American-Born Confused Desi.' Doesn't that sound like you?" asked Dad, sliding the paneer cubes into the sizzling oil.

"Okay," I said, starting to feel a little guilty. "I get it. I won't say that word again. It's not nice."

"And it's not right," added Dad. "This is America. There are people from all over the world living here. You're not more American than Avantika. If that's the case, then

Noah's more American than you because his grandparents immigrated here, not his parents."

"Well, he kind of is," I said.

Dad shook his head. "No. He isn't. That's not how it works."

"Nobody is looking at me, and definitely not at Avantika, and saying, 'Oh, she's as American as apple pie.'"

"You're as American as . . . as paneer pie," Dad said, turning the cubes in the oil.

"Well, that doesn't make me feel great. Paneer pie doesn't even exist."

Dad sighed. "My point is, you're both American. You don't have to look a certain way or sound a certain way for that to be true."

"Like after the flood in the Carolinas," said Aai. "When that temple opened its doors to all the victims, feeding and housing them. Remember that story in the *International Indian News*? Those people who always assumed anyone who looked a certain way was bad were suddenly seeing us differently. They even called the Indians there patriots, remember?"

I nodded, not sure what that had to do with our new neighbors.

"So don't be the *C* in ABCD anymore," said Dad, laughing at his own joke.

"As long as you promise not to make paneer pie," I said, patting Dad's shoulder. "It sounds disgusting."

◎   ◎

By the time the doorbell finally rang, I had finished off a lot of my candy and stashed the rest in the cupboard. I hoped that with it out of sight, my parents wouldn't remember to offer it to anyone. Dad opened the door, welcoming Avantika and her parents, Deepika Auntie and Vikram Uncle, into the house for dinner.

Every grown-up was an "auntie" or "uncle" to Indians. It made things easy when you forgot someone's name. But I had a feeling we would be seeing a lot more of this particular auntie and uncle, so I made sure to say their names in my head over and over so I wouldn't forget.

Deepika Auntie, short with sleek hair that she wore tied half up with a gold clip and then braided together just below her shoulder, gave me a huge hug.

Vikram Uncle, who was bald except for a few patches of black hair left on the sides, bent down to remove his shoes.

"I was so happy to see another Marathi family here when you introduced yourselves last night."

"I meant to ask you what your building name was in Bandra," said Aai.

"Parvati Hills," replied Vikram Uncle. Apartment buildings had names in India, to make them easier to find.

I watched as my parents and the Savarkars went back and forth with people's names until one was a winner. It turned out the woman who lived in the flat above Vikram Uncle's in Mumbai was Aai's mother's brother's sister-in-law. I wasn't surprised. Even with a billion people living in India, somehow or another my parents were almost always able to find some distant person in common with any new Indian person they met. That was just the Desi way. *Well, that and sparkly stuff, of course*, I thought as I stared at Avantika's gaudy gold seashell clip.

We led the Savarkar family down the hall and into the dining room.

"It smells so good in here!" Deepika Auntie said. She was Gujarati and pronounced English words differently than my parents did.

I inhaled deeply. The whole house was full of the smell

of the sizzling garlic from Dad's paneer, layered with the spicy blend of turmeric, mustard seeds, cumin seeds, and chili powder that Aai had cooked with. I took my seat next to Avantika.

She smiled at me and nervously tucked her hair back, opening the gold seashell clip to snap it in place.

I smiled back, but the grin quickly faded when I thought of how Harper would probably laugh at that clip tomorrow at school, or how Liam would most likely mock her accent, or how everyone would ask her where her dot was.

Before I could worry about it anymore, Aai served us the traditional Marathi meal of varan, bhaat, bhaji, and poli. Split yellow mung beans pressure-cooked into a hot varan were poured onto the basmati bhaat. It was topped off with a spoonful of toop, the Marathi word for ghee. Today's bhaji was made from bitter gourd, and the poli was steaming hot, the way the Indian flatbread tasted best. Next to it was a small bit of kairi lonche, made from pickling raw mangos, and a slice of lime with some sea salt. There was also a bowl of koshimbir, cucumber and roasted cumin powder in yogurt. And to top it all, there was Dad's totally-not-Marathi, Punjabi-style paneer.

"Oh, thank goodness," said Vikram Uncle. "I was so worried it would be nothing but Halloween candy."

"Vikram!" Deepika Auntie elbowed him hard.

Dad shook his head, smiling. "No, no. It's funny. And I bet Lekha would have been thrilled if that really were the case."

I mouthed "ha-ha" to Dad, and got a little nervous about my Halloween jackpot being handed out to make Avantika feel welcome.

"Well, we don't have chocolate bhaji, but I'm sure Lekha would be happy to give Avantika some of her Halloween candy from last night. She has more than enough."

More than enough? I couldn't believe Dad. He knew I lived under Aai's ridiculous health-food rules, and Halloween was one of the few times she let me eat what I wanted. But our neighbors were our guests, and in addition to liking shiny things, Desis like respect. So all I could do was smile and nod and hope Dad and Avantika would forget about my sugar stash.

"This looks good," I said, changing the subject as I shifted my plate. I was about to dig in but had to remove the cilantro sprinkled all over my meal first. I began my ritual surgery, pulling the green fans of cilantro leaves out of the food with my fingers and spoon and wiping them to the side of my plate.

"You don't like cilantro?" asked Avantika, watching what I was doing.

I wiped a yogurt-covered finger on the cotton napkin next to my stainless-steel plate. "I can't stand it."

"Not even in bhel?"

"That's her favorite food," said Dad. "She's always begging us to make it for her."

I shrugged. "It's okay in bhel because the chutney hides the taste."

"I read some people think it tastes like soap," added Avantika.

"To me it just tastes like barf."

Aai stifled a laugh as she finished her sip of water. "That reminds me of when Lekha was little. I had made a huge tray of barfi for Diwali. She came into the kitchen asking me what smelled so good. I told her it was barfi and asked if she wanted some. She began to cry. 'I don't want to eat barf! Don't make me eat barf!'"

Everyone at the table started laughing. I was embarrassed but couldn't help but giggle at the memory. Aai had to explain to me it's "buhr-fee" and she wasn't mispronouncing "barfy."

"I'm so glad we have neighbors like you," said Deepika Auntie in between spoonfuls of koshimbir, her diamond nose ring twinkling like a star. "When I first accepted the job at the clinic, I thought there would be so many other Indian doctors there."

Dad shook his head with a small smile. "Just me. And your office is several floors away."

"Yeah," Deepika Auntie continued. "And I didn't realize we would be so far away from all the Indian organizations in Detroit."

Aai nodded. "It's an hour away. We probably don't go there as often as we should. But I'm happy the girls will have each other now. Kids here want to grow up so fast, shaving and wearing makeup so early. They don't get time to enjoy being kids. . . ." She glanced at Avantika's empty plate. "Ankhin kaay pahije, Avantika?" Aai asked, uncovering the dishes to find out what else Avantika wanted to eat. "Oh, sorry, Deepika. You're not Marathi. I wasn't thinking. What language do you all speak at home?"

"Mala donhi bhasha yetat, Auntie," said Avantika, telling Aai she was fluent in both Gujarati *and* Marathi.

Dad gave me a triumphant look, and I began to tear at what was left of my poli, crumbling the bread on my plate. He was right. I was wrong, and mean, to have laughed about Avantika's accent.

"But I'm fine, Auntie. The food was excellent," Avantika continued.

"You're a growing child. Besides, it's your first time here. How about some paneer?"

"No, it's okay. Really," she added, waving her hands over her empty plate.

Too late. Aai was already putting paneer on the plate in the gap under Avantika's hands. She then took a scoop of koshimbir and filled the steel bowl next to the paneer.

Avantika sighed and smiled, and began to eat with a humble "thank you."

Aai was a master at the timeless Marathi art of aagrah, where you forced someone to take a second or third helping because it was the gracious thing to do. You never wanted your guest to leave your home on an empty stomach. I was aagrah'd really bad once on my last trip to India. I was just eight and we were at my cousin's Seemant Pujan, where the groom is welcomed by the bride's family before the wedding. His fiancée's relatives kept giving me syrupy jilbi after syrupy jilbi. I kept saying no, but they kept serving me throughout the evening. By dinner, I had eaten twenty-one jilbis, and then spent the meal puking in a corner. I was the definition of "barfy."

"Ani, Lekha?" Vikram Uncle asked me, motioning to the plates. "Kordi poli khau nakos."

The parents and Avantika smiled at the dry poli I was eating, my bhaji done. My ears started to feel hot even though I wasn't calling my aaji in India. "I'm fine. Thanks," I mumbled, avoiding eye contact with Avantika just in case she was trying not to laugh at me for answering in English instead of Marathi.

"No problem," replied Uncle. "Avantika, tell your friend what your classes are tomorrow. Maybe you have some in common."

I listened as Avantika spouted off the memorized schedule. She was in eighth-grade math and science. Even though I was a straight-A student, I was not two grades ahead in any subject, so we definitely did not have those together. But we did have English together in the morning, B lunch together in the afternoon, and PE together after that.

Deepika Auntie put her hands in a namaskar and looked up at the ceiling, "Oh, thank God. I'm so glad you'll have your friend with you tomorrow, Avantika. You'll take care of your friend, won't you, Lekha?"

"Of course," Uncle chimed in, speaking for me. "Why wouldn't she? They're going to be best friends."

I nodded, glancing at Avantika, who gave me an apologetic smile. I thought about everything Avantika was going to go through tomorrow. How I wouldn't have the courage to stick up for her since I didn't have any to stand up for myself, let alone a stranger at school. How everyone was going to assume we were friends because we were both Indian. How Liam and Harper would react to her. Before I knew it, I felt an uneasy, nervous quiver deep down, like the one I had felt just before getting sick from all that aagrah in India. I guess the feeling was fitting, since this sort of felt like aagrah, being force-fed a friendship I just wasn't interested in.

chapter FIVE

I went to school the next morning, sleepy, cranky, and nervous from a restless night of worrying about Avantika at school. I suppose I should have been grateful, though. Aai had offered to drive Avantika when she took Noah and me to school, but Uncle and Auntie wanted to take her to her first day of school themselves. I wasn't sure my nerves could handle entering school with Avantika.

I passed the empty student desk next to the teacher's desk and took my front-row seat in Mr. Crowe's English class, right next to Noah. He had spent the entire drive asking me about Avantika and wondering if she would agree to let him write a "Meet the New Student" piece on her for the paper. Anything for a cover story, I guess.

Liam entered the room, seemingly recovered from not making the swim team. He took his seat behind me.

"What reeks?" he muttered, popping some Junior Mints into his mouth.

Sometimes I hated questions. Because with just one, Liam was able to make me feel like a disgusting outsider who was beneath him. With just one question, he was able to leave me speechless, and not in a good way, like when I saw that I beat my own swimming record. This was in the bad way. In the no-words-are-coming-out-and-I-just-want-a-sinkhole-to-appear-in-the-ground-and-swallow-me-up way.

I quickly made sure my hair was still in place, swept over my forehead and birthmark, and looked down at my desk, trying to sniff the collar of my turtleneck without being obvious. Had the smell of all the sizzling spices from dinner come for a ride on my sweater? I couldn't tell, but I hoped if the bad smell was coming from my clothes, no one else would notice it.

"Is it you, Dot?" Liam asked, fanning his nose as he scooted between the desks and made his way past me.

I turned to Noah, but he was staring hard at his fingers, as if he were noticing them for the first time. I knew what he was doing, though. We always just avoided eye contact when one of us was being teased and stood there in silence as if we weren't there. It was just less embarrassing that way if your best friend wasn't witnessing your humiliation.

But other kids were witnessing it. I chewed on the insides of my cheeks, watching apprehensively as more classmates piled in, easing up my bite when no one else scrunched their face in my direction. Avantika was the last to enter. She was wearing her gold seashell hair clip. I sank in my seat, but her tense shoulders relaxed when she saw me.

Mr. Crowe, who had been waiting by the door reading a piece of paper, ushered Avantika to the front of the room. "All right, gang, hope you're all recovered from Halloween. We have a new student joining us today. Her family just moved here from Bombay—sorry. Mum-baay," he said, mispronouncing "Mumbai." "So let's give a warm welcome to . . ."

Mr. Crowe stared at the piece of paper in his hands as I waited for him to butcher Avantika's name. I also tried to figure out how Avantika would attempt to correct his pronunciation in the game of Indian-name charades every Desi kid is all too familiar with. *"Aah-vaahn-TEE-ka?" "No, Mr. Crowe. It's Uh (like if you were scratching your chin while you were thinking), VUHNT (with your tongue behind your top teeth to make the* t *sound), ih (like the beginning of "in"), kah (like the snake in* Jungle Book*)."*

But there was no game of charades. Because despite thinking my name was pronounced "Lee-kha," Mr. Crowe said Avantika's name almost perfectly, just shy of saying the *t* sound correctly.

"Avantika," he said again. "That was my college roommate's mom's name."

I was shocked. Maybe Mr. Crowe had more experience with different cultures than I thought. Maybe he was cooler than I thought.

He ran his fingers through his blond curls and pulled the empty student desk right next to mine, its steel feet groaning as they scratched the hard floor. "Come on in and have a seat, Avantika. I think you'll be very comfortable with Lekha here to help you."

Nope. I was wrong. He wasn't cooler than I thought. Putting Avantika next to the only other brown kid in the class was the furthest thing from cool he could do. Noah frowned as he mouthed "racist?" to me. Liam and some other kids behind me snickered, while Avantika took her seat. She raised an eyebrow at me over Mr. Crowe's segregationist seating assignment. I gave a small shrug back. It was pretty absurd that Mr. Crowe thought the two Desis had to sit next to each other. But on the other hand, maybe he really did think Avantika could use a familiar face.

"So, tell us about yourself, Avantika," Mr. Crowe said, sitting backward in his chair.

"Well . . ." Avantika's voice shook a little as she began. Liam coughing at her "well" that sounded like "vell" didn't seem to be helping her nerves either.

Great. It was already happening. People were laughing at her. And I bet they were laughing at me, too, thinking that's how my parents said their *W*s. And thanks to *our* parents, I was going to be stuck with this all year, guilty by association. I wanted to shout, "That's not how my parents sound!" But instead, I just slouched farther down in my seat as Avantika continued.

"I used to live in a flat by the sea."

"A flat what?" asked Emma from the far side of the room, not bothering to look up from a doodle she was drawing in the margin of her notebook, probably of goose poop.

"*Flat* means 'apartment,'" Mr. Crowe interjected. "It's a

British word. India used to be ruled by the British. Isn't that right, Avantika?"

"That's right. Just like America was."

Mr. Crowe stood up, his face turning a little pink. "Right. Of course. Er, how about three more interesting facts about yourself?"

"I used to play field hockey at my old school; I do Bharat Natyam, which is a classical Indian dance; and I had a dog named Ram, who used to love to drink chai with me."

"I love chai tea," added Mr. Crowe.

Avantika gave me a small smile. I could tell she wanted to correct our teacher and let him know "chai" was "tea," so "chai tea" was "tea tea," but she was holding back to be polite. But I had been hearing people talk about chai tea my whole life and didn't feel the need to have an inside joke with someone I barely knew and was so different from. So I didn't return the smile. Instead, I focused on drawing a cow in my notebook, and hoped Avantika wouldn't expect me to always be by her side to help her understand how things worked here.

"Thanks so much for sharing a little about yourself, Avantika," said Mr. Crowe, returning to his desk. "I hope you'll all be open to digging deep and sharing more of your-selves, because this year I want everyone to write a short op-ed for the school paper. It's my goal that you understand the power of your own voice through this assignment. Each month, three of your op-eds will go in the paper, and if it's really good, it's going to be on the front page."

Front page. I looked over as Noah began to drum his fingers on his desk with excitement. He was getting a racing-thoughts look in his wide eyes, kind of like Cookie when we asked her if she wanted to go on a walk.

"You can check the class portal to find out what month you're assigned to. So start thinking about what you want to say. The December paper is just a few weeks away. And from the looks of it, Mr. Wade, you already know what yours will be about."

"I'm going to write about Abigail Winters," Noah said.

A small groan went through the back of the class, but Noah just spoke louder, his voice getting higher pitched as his enthusiasm grew.

"About how Senator Osher got sick and had to step down, the special election in January, and how Winters is blaming immigrants for taking auto jobs from everyone."

I felt my classmates' eyes on me, but I snuck a glance at Avantika, the only immigrant in the room. Her ears were starting to flush the same color as the red powdery kunku Aai kept in front of the gods in our devghar, our home temple.

"That's great," said Mr. Crowe. "But the way you described it, it's just an article. You have to figure out what your personal stake is in this. And what the story means to you."

Liam's hand shot up. "If you let him say something about Winters, you have to let someone else say something about Sharpe. It's the law."

"That's not exactly the law, but I'm all for showing both sides of the argument and the political spectrum," said Mr. Crowe, opening the English book in front of him.

"Good," said Liam. "Because my dad said immigrants have the press eating out of their hands."

"Liam," warned Mr. Crowe.

"My parents and I don't have anyone eating out of our hands," said Avantika, punctuating her point with a pencil jab to her desk.

I couldn't believe it. She was talking back to Liam, defending herself.

"That's funny. Cuz you guys eat with your hands," Liam retorted.

"Enough," said Mr. Crowe, walking toward our desks.

"What about free speech? Freedom of the press?" asked Liam.

"It's okay, Mr. Crowe," said Avantika, turning to face Liam. "Do you not eat with your hands here?"

Liam snorted in disbelief and shook his head. "No. We're not weird."

"So, you eat sandwiches with a knife and fork here in Michigan? And bananas and oranges and popcorn? I guess I could learn to do whatever your local custom is, however weird it may be."

Liam just stood there, speechless.

She had done it. She didn't need me to defend her. She had done it herself. I stared at Avantika in awe, and for a second there I wished I did have some food in my hands. A sandwich, poli, bhaji, whatever, even if everyone thought it stank. Because then I could give my mouth something to do other than hang open in total shock.

chapter
SIX

I tried hard to picture myself standing up to a bully the way Avantika had in the morning as I headed down the ramp to the cafeteria with Noah. I tried, but I couldn't. I didn't know how I'd stop my voice from shaking. Or what witty comeback I'd say. Or how loud I'd say it.

Trying not to get trampled by the eighth graders who towered over me, the seventh graders who towered over me, or my fellow sixth graders, who also towered over me, I sped up, attempting to keep up with the flow. I slid my finger up and down the handle of my midnight-blue lunch bag. I knew right where a little strand of thread stuck out around the bend, from when my handle had gotten snagged on my locker. I'd had the bag since third grade, and aside from the locker mishap, it looked like new. Even better than that, though, it was familiar. I dealt with enough unknowns from Liam and other kids in town. I didn't need any more surprises. I didn't do well with change.

I sat down at our corner table right by the ramp wall, under one of the many posters in our school that said, in huge bright letters, KINDNESS IS KOOL! Noah, who complained about this spelling of "cool" at least once a week, set down his water bottle and headed across the cafeteria. He had to buy his lunch from crabby Mrs. Finch, the lunch lady with the gray bun that was pulled too tight under her hairnet. She always seemed almost as repulsed by the hot lunch as the students were.

Aai seemed to agree. She never let me buy lunch. She said it was a waste of money, and the vegetarian selection was always gross. And besides, she liked to add, it was full of processed ingredients and chemicals, unlike the organic lunches she packed for me. Dad constantly reminded Aai that no one had dropped dead from eating an unorganic meal before. He told her we ate plenty of nonorganic food like Indian grains and lentils and meals at restaurants, but she still insisted that I never buy lunch at school.

I unzipped my bag and opened up my stainless-steel lunch box, revealing, surprise surprise, the same meal I had eaten almost every day of school: a peanut butter and jelly sandwich, apple slices, carrots, cucumbers, and homemade yogurt with berries. But the sandwich was raised on one end, like something was stuck underneath it. I lifted it up to peek, and sure enough, there were two little, wrapped chocolate squares. Dad had raided my stash. And the two pieces were probably his not-so-subtle reminder to share.

I held the squares in my hand as I scanned the cafeteria for Avantika, thinking about how disappointed Dad would have been if he knew I was avoiding her. I squeezed my hand and felt the squares wobble limply. The heat from my fingers was melting them, turning them soft. I opened one up. Brown was smeared across the wrapper. It wasn't a good look. And it would have been gross to give Avantika some warm, half-melted chocolate that Emma could have used as a model for one of her bird-poop masterpieces. So I quickly tore at the other square's wrapper and popped both pieces of chocolate into my mouth.

With dessert done, I dug in, taking a bite of the PBJ. I worked my way around the lunch box clockwise as I watched

Noah make his way through the line. Behind him, under a busted cafeteria light that flickered endlessly, sat Emma, at a small table by herself. Several cliques and tables over, Harper sat with a bunch of girls wearing shaded lip tints Aai would never let me wear. They were giggling into their hands about something. At the table behind them, Liam was running from seat to seat, screaming, "Lice!" as he tapped each guy on the head and they jokingly swatted at him. Liam happened to look in my direction during what looked like a choreographed spin before he drummed his fingers on his friend Mikey's blond buzz cut. But I turned away quickly, checking that my hair was in place, hoping to not give Liam another opportunity to stick his finger to his forehead when he saw me.

And that's when I saw Noah walking toward our spot, Avantika by his side. It had been two class periods since I had seen her last. I'd worried about our next encounter throughout math and science. Trying to hide my embarrassment that we would be eating together and be kind instead (because it was "kool"), I smiled at her, scooching over a bit so she would have room to sit.

Noah and I always sat together. It was always just the two of us, even when we were in elementary school and sat at a table with our class. Noah and I sat on the end, and despite the twenty other kids sitting near us, it felt like it was just the two of us talking about our favorite dogs in second grade, our favorite books in third grade, our favorite dragons in fourth grade, and plans to start a class newspaper in fifth grade, back when I was as interested in having others read my writing as Noah was. But until Avantika made friends of her own, of course she would be sitting with us.

I watched her open up a brown paper bag. The top had been wrinkled limp, like someone had twisted it too hard all day. Avantika caught my eye.

"I got a little nervous when I saw all these kids I didn't know and couldn't find you guys," she said. "Guess I took it out on the bag. So much for reusing it. I hope my mom doesn't make me bring my next meal in an old yogurt container."

I couldn't help but smile. It was almost Indian tradition to reuse yogurt containers to send food home from parties with the guests. Aai used to do it too on the rare occasion someone from Detroit was in town, stopping by on their way to another city. But then she saw some news story about plastics leaching chemicals into food, and that was the end of that little custom in our house.

Avantika's mom must not have gotten the "Plastics Will Poison Us All" memo. I watched as she opened an old plastic take-out container, revealing two small methi parathas, round flatbread made with bitter fenugreek and spiced with cumin and cayenne. Methi parathas were my favorite weekend lunch, but I would never have brought them to school. Why ask for that kind of attention? Did she want someone to loudly ask what the stink was? Or people to exchange disgusted looks as she ate it?

Before I could even think about a nice way to warn Avantika about the hazards of bringing Indian food to school, she pulled a little plastic container of tamarind chutney out of her bag. I shoved a cucumber slice in my mouth and pretended not to be eyeing her food, but I had to know what she was eating chincha chutney with. Was it bhel? My absolute favorite? Samosas, my second favorite? Or was she just going to down the chutney, my unorthodox, third favorite way to eat chincha chutney? She grabbed a misshapen lump of aluminum foil out of her bag, and I had my answer. Samosas.

The smell from the little pyramids of fried dough filled with potatoes and peas hit me. And it smelled good. Not too spicy. Just the right amount of ova. Just like when we ate at What's the Mattar?, the Indian restaurant forty-five minutes from our house. It was the only time other than parties and Diwali when Aai would let me eat as much fried food as I wanted.

Avantika dipped the triangular point of the samosa into the chutney and bit into the crunchy, flaky crust as I chewed on the last bite of neglected PBJ crust. I would have given anything to swap places with Avantika right then.

"What's your friend eating, Dot?" asked Liam as he and Mikey walked by us to throw their trash out.

I fiddled with my lunch-box latch, trying to ignore the question, hoping there wouldn't be more.

"Yeah, it reeks," added Mikey with a gag, putting a finger in his mouth. "And where's her dot?"

Liam strummed his fingers on Mikey's head, fluttering them down until just his index finger remained. He dramatically pointed at the center of Mikey's forehead.

Noah's ears turned red. He looked down at his food uncomfortably like he always did when Liam made fun of me. I stared at my reflection in my lunch box and chewed extra slowly on that last bite of crust, even though most of it was already down my throat. But Avantika just looked straight at the boys and shrugged.

"Why're you bugging her? Just ask me. It's a samosa. You'd like it if you tried it," she added, waving the half-eaten samosa near them so fast a pea flew out of it, bopping Liam in the head.

Mikey tapped on Liam's head as they headed back to their table. "Looks like you're the one with lice now, bro!"

Avantika rolled her eyes and continued to eat, unbothered. "Are they always like that?"

I squeezed the handle of my lunch bag hard, realizing I had an answer, just not to Avantika's question. I had an answer to my question from the beginning of lunch. I knew exactly how loud my voice would be when facing a bully.

It would be totally silent.

chapter SEVEN

*A*fter lunch Avantika and I turned the corner from the cafeteria toward the gym. I ignored the looks from the other kids, gawking at the only two Desis in school walking together. Black hair, brown skin, one with an accent and one without. Did they think we were a perfect match? Related? The exact same?

"They're probably wondering who cloned me," I muttered as we entered the gym.

"Who are?" asked Avantika.

"Nothing." I scowled at the yellow lights reflecting off the maple floor. I was strong from swimming, but I still hated PE. I hated having to smack a volleyball with my tender hands, hands that were used to being cradled by pool water.

I despised having to kick a soccer ball with tired feet that were better suited for propelling me forward like a shark in the ocean. And most of all, I dreaded dancing.

I was one of those rare Indian girls who was not coordinated enough for Bharat Natyam, Kathak, or folk dance. My parents had me try all of them in our long, weekend drives down to Detroit in elementary school. But I got sick of trying to keep up with the other kids and even sicker of apologizing every time I bumped into them. After a couple of months Aai realized it was a wonder I could even manage doing raas. She took pity on me and let me quit. It gave me more time to work on my Bollywood dance moves in my room. That way no one would watch as I shook my hips while accidentally shaking my bookshelves and spun in circles, sending my swimming trophies spinning to the ground in their own Bollywood twirls.

Unfortunately for me, today in PE, Mr. Jennings was all about line dancing. "Footloose" was already blaring. A couple of kids practiced while I showed Avantika the locker room. We headed for the cluster of green lockers surrounded by rows of black lockers, our school's colors.

"Did you bring a lock?"

Avantika nodded, pulling a blue lock out of her backpack pocket.

I pointed to the locker next to mine. "This one is empty."

Avantika took her gym clothes out. "You mean, you just change here? In front of everyone?"

It was the first time I had seen Avantika look so nervous, and imagined this is what her poor paper bag saw before she crumpled it up.

I nodded, holding up my blue shirt. It wasn't fun, but that's just how it was. "Turn your back to everyone else, and tuck your arms into your shirt. Then put your hands into your new shirt and quickly change," I said, showing Avantika the fastest method to change without everyone looking at your body.

She took out her gym clothes, which strangely enough also consisted of a blue shirt and black shorts, and followed my lead.

"Now pull your shirt down over your butt and change out of your pants."

I pulled my jeans down and rapidly moved into my pair of black shorts, my arm brushing against the fine hairs on my leg. Just then, Harper walked by us with Aidy, a sixth grader from the other elementary school in town, who I had just met at the beginning of the school year.

"Hey, Lekha." Harper smiled as she walked to her locker, pulling her sweater over her head and slipping into her gym shorts.

Avantika bit her lip as she made a disapproving clicking noise with her tongue that made me feel like Aai were here. "Maybe you should teach her your way," she said, staring at Harper.

I pulled Avantika out of the locker room, thinking maybe I should have taught *her* about whispering.

The singer on Mr. Jennings's phone could have learned a thing or two about using an indoor voice too. He was wailing about being footloose while Mr. Jennings was showing the class the rest of the line dance we had been practicing last week.

"Ah!" Mr. Jennings danced over to us. "Lekha and Aven . . . Ah-vin . . . ka?"

"Avantika," we both said.

Avantika gave me a small smile.

"Right. What you said. It will take me a while, but I'll get it."

I doubted that. Mr. Jennings still couldn't say my name right after all these weeks of school, and he definitely didn't bother trying to learn the right way, either. It just wasn't important enough. So I had to go through years of everyone at school butchering my name because it was easier that way. And every time someone said my name in attendance, or in the hall, or during a group assignment, it was the perfect reminder of how different I was.

"Welcome to PE," Mr. Jennings continued. "Let's start dancing." He shimmied back to the front of the class, probably grateful he didn't have to take a test on pronouncing Avantika's name.

I took a deep breath and joined the back line, Avantika by my side, as Harper and the rest of the girls emerged from the locker room to take their places next to us. We crisscrossed, shuffled, jumped from heel to toe, slid, and clapped. I was always a split second off, and my crisscross was sometimes more of a step-on-Avantika's-toes-and-say-sorry. But I started to get the hang of it. Avantika had no issues.

"This is kind of like the dances in those nineties movies," she huffed as she spun with ease. "You know, the ones with Govinda?"

I shook my head as hard as I was shaking my shoulders, and caught Harper's eye. I desperately wished Avantika would stop talking about Indian things in front of everyone.

"You haven't seen them? The songs had Govinda and whoever the heroine was dancing side by side, sometimes in front of European stores with hundreds of white people staring into the camera in the background as they watched. So just channel your inner Govinda," said Avantika as she clapped and whooped right when she was supposed to, tipping her imaginary hat.

I almost fell forward while reaching for my imaginary hat, which must have been flung halfway across the gym by this point from my ungraceful moves.

"Nice work, Lekha!" shouted Mr. Jennings.

What was nice about my tripping? But then I realized he was looking at Avantika.

"I think he thinks you're me," I panted, trying to keep up with her.

"No," Avantika replied as we turned to dance in the opposite direction. "You're doing a great job. He's just complimenting you—"

Mr. Jennings began to wave his hands at Avantika.

"Come to the front, Lekha! Looks like you kicked off your Sunday shoes! You've got this!"

Avantika gasped. "You're right! It's like *Seeta Aur Geeta*!" She paused. "Sorry. You probably don't get that reference either."

But I did get it. It was a funny old Hindi movie where twins got separated at birth and then switched places as adults and got even with people who were mean to them. In fact, it was one of many twins-separated-at-birth movies with the same plot, and I had seen them all with Dad. They were our favorites.

"Or like *Ram Aur Shyam*," I said with a small smile.

"Or *Kishen Kanhaiya*," laughed Avantika, almost testing me.

"Or *ChaalBaaz* with Anju and Manju." I grinned. "That's my favorite."

"Mine too!" whispered Avantika.

"Let's go, Lekha! To the front!" called Mr. Jennings.

"You'd better go, Anju," I said to Avantika.

She winked as she ran up to the front. "Bye, Manju."

I fumbled to the music, watching "Lekha's" gold seashell clip bop along to the beat at the front of the class. I bent my knee up, supposing we really did all look the same to some people, and swung my heel from side to side, accidentally knocking into Harper.

Before I could apologize, Aidy bent down giggling, staring at my leg.

"Did the broom get you?" she whispered loudly to Harper.

I looked down at my leg. At the little black hairs on it.

Broom. A new nickname. As if Dot weren't bad enough. I blinked quickly, wishing I hadn't heard that question. Was nothing about me acceptable to people like Aidy?

"Just dance, Aidy," muttered Harper, turning away from her. "Sorry, Lekha," she added softly as she clapped her hands and daintily spun her hand like she was holding a lasso.

But I just stared straight ahead in silence, my ears burning. I was tired of people mispronouncing my name, and even more tired of people calling me names. I wished that just in this moment, these girls called me the wrong name. I knew it was wrong, but I'd rather they were making fun of "Avantika" than "Lekha."

chapter
EIGHT

*T*hat evening I got a break from my twindian, thanks to swim practice. It was my first practice as a full-fledged member of the Dolphins, so I made sure we got there earlier than normal. Harper seemed to have had the same thought, because by the time I got changed and to the poolside, she was already in the water, practicing her butterfly.

"Hey, Lekha!" She waved, emerging from the ribbons of foam she had formed in the water.

"Hey." I smiled, hopping into the icy water in the shallow end, which felt as soothing to me as a warm bath. It seemed saying "Hey" was as deep as our friendship was going to get, though, when Aidy and a tall girl with wavy into the pool, their squeals echoing in the humid room as they hugged Harper.

"I knew you would make it!" said the tall girl, wrapping her hair into a bun on the top of her head and tying it in place with the thin hair tie around her wrist, a hair tie that would have snapped had it been holding my heavy hair in a ponytail.

"This is Lekha," added Harper, pointing to me. "She just made it too."

I gave a friendly nod and quickly tugged at the front of my cap, making sure my birthmark was under it.

"Awesome. I'm Kendall. I go to Hayden Village."

The private school. That's why I hadn't seen her before.

"Coach told us you guys are going to relay with us so we can finally compete in the two hundred," said Aidy, acting as if she hadn't just laughed at me a few hours earlier. "After Ellen moved and Lizzie quit for cheer, I didn't think we'd ever get a good team together, but I am so glad you guys tried out. We're going to be amazing."

I dunked my head underwater, getting my face wet, and emerged for air with a smile, adding, "So amazing." If Aidy was going to pretend nothing had happened, I could too. Bring on the selective amnesia.

Coach Turner blew his whistle and motioned for everyone to get in the pool. As the splashes died down, he sat by the edge of the water, dipping his feet in. "All right, Dolphins. We have three new teammates, so wave your flippers at Lekha, Harper, and John, and give them a warm welcome. We're going to have a great practice." Coach skimmed through the papers on his clipboard as the twenty-some members of the Dolphins exchanged "Hi"s and introductions.

"Just a couple of reminders, gang," continued Coach Turner. "Practice starts at five thirty p.m. Not five thirty-one, not five thirty-seven, and certainly not five forty-five. Five thirty sharp. Be on time to make sure you can beat the other teams' times. We have a long stretch of practices, and then you'll have Thanksgiving off and two weeks off for Christmas and New Year's. I'm not that cruel to make you practice instead of celebrating the holidays with your families."

As a few kids laughed at Coach's joke, I realized he had forgotten other holidays, including one celebrated by millions: Diwali. It wasn't his fault. It was hard to keep up with Diwali. It was based on the lunar calendar, so the dates of the five-day-long festival of lights changed every year, falling sometime between October and November. The worst was when it was the same day as Halloween, or "Diwaleen," as I liked to call it. Aai would grumble about putting up skeletons and ghosts all around the house when we were supposed to be celebrating with colorful lamps and paper lanterns. This year there was no Diwaleen, though. This year Diwali was next week.

So it turned out Coach *would* be making me practice instead of celebrating one of my family's biggest holidays. But I didn't mind. I always had to go to school and extra-curriculars during Diwali here in Michigan. The only time I had ever seen things differently was three years ago when I was in India. Diwali was right before my cousin's wedding that year.

It was bizarre to be in India and see all my cousins off work and school for a whole week. We went to the theater to see Hindi movies. We went out for ice cream, lit divas, and made powdery patterns of decorative rangoli outside doors. And we exchanged gift envelopes of money every time a new neighbor or relative showed up. It felt totally unreal to see so many people all around me celebrating Diwali with sparklers and nonstop fireworks at night, seeing almost every towering building draped in blankets of holiday lights, seeing all the stores with signs for Diwali sales. None of that happened in our small town, miles away from the large Indian American communities in Metro Detroit, and I'd never explained any of that to Coach, so how would he know?

He blew his whistle, signaling for everyone to get into their own lanes, based on what they were swimming. Harper, Aidy, Kendall, and I were in lane three. The order for the relay was different from the individual medley, so I was eager to find out what I was going to swim.

"Harper, you'll start us off with the backstroke. Kendall, you'll stick with breaststroke. Aidy, I'm moving you to fly, and Lekha, you'll be freestyle."

Aidy gave a small, sulking hop in the water. "But I always swim anchor."

"I know, Aidy, and you've always made up more than enough time for everyone. But Lekha had an incredible swim at tryouts. Her freestyle was the fastest time in the under twelves. If she can replicate that at a meet, no one will be able to touch you guys. So, come on out, team. Support each other. Remember that teammates stick together. And let's do this."

I put my elbows on the slimy tiles at the pool's edge and

pulled myself out of the water. I knew it was best to stay quiet if I wanted to get on Aidy's good side, if I wanted to fit in. So instead of telling Aidy that Coach was right and I deserved this spot, I pretended my swim cap needed adjusting, focused on my feet, and steadied my chattering teeth. Anything to avoid the icy stare from Aidy that was making me feel colder than I already was.

I backed up, almost bumping into the assistant coach, letting Kendall go ahead of me. Harper got in the pool, hands holding the edge, in position to start the backstroke. The whistle blew. She flung herself back into the pool and began to kick her way to the far end. She tapped and turned back toward us. The water seemed to slide away from her, creating a diagonal pattern off her swim cap. As she tapped the side of the pool we were on, Kendall dove in over her, swiftly doing the breaststroke.

"Faster, Kenny!" shouted Aidy. "You're slowing us down!"

"Give her a sec, Aidy. New teams take a few practices to gel," said Coach gently, checking the clock.

"She's always been on breaststroke. I'm the one doing something totally new."

Aidy dove in as Kendall tapped the edge. Her butterfly

was fast. Much faster than mine. From the starting block, I watched as Aidy splashed through the pool, turned, and made her way toward me. My belly began to flutter and my palms started to sweat. Aidy tapped the edge and I dove in.

My arms cut through the water as I kicked forward. I tried to focus on my form as I turned, but all I could think about was that I had to show Aidy how good I was. I felt more and more nervous with each arc of my arms, until I finally tapped the wall, back with my relay team.

"A couple of seconds off, kiddo," said Coach Turner. "Keep practicing. You'll get it," he added as he headed to the next lane.

My time was more than a couple of seconds off. It was almost six seconds off. I had choked. Instead of swimming the anchor leg, I had let Aidy get into my head so badly, it was like I had swum with an anchor tied to my leg.

Aidy's face was so red, she couldn't even speak. Kendall seemed to be relieved Aidy was focusing her anger on me instead of her. And Harper just gave me a look of pity as I treaded water in the pool, my team looking down at me. All I could do was stare at the pool water, where I had failed my team. Where was that selective amnesia when I needed it?

chapter
NINE

I tried not to think about my disastrous practice the rest of the week and concentrated instead on cobwebs and dust. The five days of Diwali were kicked off with a weekend of nonstop cleaning, with breaks for homework and meals.

"Everyone has a clean house for Diwali, and we aren't going to be any different," said Aai, having just returned from Avantika's house and seeing all their boxes unpacked and belongings put away.

So Dad was forced to go through his months-old mail mountains that were placed between all the plants in the Jungle. Aai vacuumed. And I was on cobweb-demolition duty, apologizing to each little blond spider as I destroyed its hard work.

Maybe I could write an op-ed about spiderwebs, I thought as I finished removing the sticky cobweb curtains in the basement near Dad's picture of the lotus-shaped Baha'i temple. That would for sure spare me the front page of the paper early next year when mine was due. If only I could think of a point of view. Was I pro-spiderweb or anti? I wondered as I headed past the kitchen counter with our devghar on it, wiping it off, dusting around the idols.

When Aai worked at her engineering job, we briefly had a cleaning lady. But one day Aai found a four-inch silver idol of the goddess Lakshmi in the trash. The cleaning lady said she thought it was an old action figure so she'd tossed it, and Aai decided to never again have a stranger clean the house.

With our home now as spotless as Avantika's, and Dad's mail mountains now more like mail hills, our house was finally Diwali-clean. Dad and Aai started making dinner and Diwali faraal, the sweet and savory fried snacks munched on throughout the holiday.

I watched as Dad churned the handle on the stainless-steel tube of the chakli maker over a small kadhai, an iron bowl that was filled with oil for frying on the stove. The chakli maker pressed the dough made from lentil and rice flours into a star-shaped noodle that Dad then swirled into a spiky pinwheel in the crackling oil.

Aai was cutting diagonal lines into two rolled-out masses of dough that looked like misshapen continents. One was savory dough spiced with carom seeds. The other was sweet dough. She prepped the diamond-shaped khari shankarpali and shankarpali for frying next.

I licked my lips, impatient for the meal, as I did the rangoli. The decorations made of colored powder, flowers, bangles, or lentils and grains were put outside doors and in the house for Diwali. I was making Ganpati out of yellow mung, using white basmati rice for his tusks and red lentils for his pants and crown. Aai had already made an intricate rangoli design using rice she had dyed with plant-based food coloring. It had purple and green paisleys and red flowers. In the center was a large swastik made out of baby bangles.

This was Aai's favorite design. It was painted at the doorway of her house and several homes in her neighborhood. It stood for luck and for God. It reminded her of home and of making large swastik rangolis with her aai in India when she was a kid. It was a huge, ancient Hindu symbol of auspiciousness from thousands of years ago, used in pujas, weddings, and holidays, found in temples and in almost every Hindu home. My relatives even gave me gold swastik necklaces when we visited them. But despite what it meant in India, I had to beg Aai to stop putting it on the porch in Michigan, because the symbol had been turned diagonal by Hitler and now had a terrible meaning everywhere besides India. I was tired of explaining to Noah that we weren't Nazis. And I was embarrassed at seeing the horrified looks on trick-or-treaters' faces during Diwaleen when they saw the swastik on the porch. So Aai finally moved the design indoors a couple of years ago.

With my rangoli done, I started stringing Diwali lights up on the master bedroom window. Aai and Dad's room faced the street, and I loved how the lights looked from outside. I steadied myself on a stepstool and twisted the lights around the silver tinsel with dangling paisleys that Aai had already put there, cherished decor from our last shopping expedition in India during Diwali.

I plugged the lights in and marveled at the pink, green, orange, and blue reflections of the little blinking lights on the silver tinsel garland. The lights were lit. The rangoli was done. The sounds of oil popping and sputtering from the kitchen danced near my ears. And the smells of carom seeds and fried dough wafted in the air. I beamed, a happy, peaceful feeling coming over me as I took in the wonder of Diwali.

☙ ❧

The next day in English class I was dressed in the nonfestive outfit of a fuzzy alien-green sweater with gray corduroys, my hair over my bindi birthmark. Avantika was wearing real gold bangles and an olive-green sweater with a mustard-yellow odhani with gold sequins and orange flowers embroidered on it. And on her forehead, she had an actual bindi.

"Happy Diwali, Lekha and Avantika," said Mr. Crowe, putting his hands together in a namaste that made me feel really embarrassed for him.

"Thanks," I said, anxiously crossing and uncrossing my feet under the desk. I knew what was coming next. It happened whenever a teacher remembered it was Diwali, which, annoyingly and yet thankfully, wasn't often. It was time for Ambassador Lekha, representing the great land of India, to give a lecture on a holiday celebrated differently by millions of people in thirty seconds, the maximum amount of time people could politely pretend to be interested in stuff that made no sense to them.

"So how about you tell the class a little about your holiday, Lekha?"

There it was. "It's the festival of lights," I responded, turning to Noah, who gave me a somewhat supportive shrug-smile. "It's also some people's new year."

"It isn't everyone's?" Emma asked from the back.

I bit the inside of my cheeks. Another question meant another minute that my torture was prolonged. But I had no answer to this question because I had no idea why. All I knew was that for my family, the new year was in the spring, during a holiday called Gudhi Padwa.

"India is really diverse, with lots of religions and traditions," said Avantika, playing with her odhani. "Each state speaks a different language, in addition to English, and they have their own customs. So while the Hindu new year does start during Diwali for some people, it doesn't for others. Like, it is the new year for my Gujarati side but not for my Marathi side."

Liam snorted from the back, and I tried to send a telepathic note to Ambassador Avantika to stop her speech, since no one here knew what she was talking about.

"Do you have a question, Liam?" asked Mr. Crowe.

"Nope."

Avantika ran her fingers through her shiny hair, bangles jingling as she continued. "Several different religions celebrate Diwali. In Jainism, Diwali is the day Bhagwan Mahavir attained moksha, the end of the cycle of rebirth."

I avoided everyone's glances and stared at Avantika as hard as I could, trying to get her attention. *Hello? Earth to Avantika. Stop the speech.*

"Many Hindus celebrate it as Ram's return from exile after defeating the demon king, Ravan."

Can you hear me? Is this thing on? I cleared my throat loudly, but the ambassador still had to give her concluding remarks.

"Basically, in many of the different ways to celebrate Diwali, it is a celebration of good over evil, symbolized by lighting lamps. That's why it is the festival of lights."

"Is that why you're wearing your dot today?" asked Liam from his desk.

"Yeah, it is. And it's not a dot. It's called a 'tikli' in Marathi. It's called 'chandlo' in Gujarati. It's called 'bindi' in Hindi. It's called 'kumkuma' in Kannada," she replied.

"It's called 'fashion' in American, Liam. You wouldn't get it," retorted Harper. "I think it's neat."

Neat. She thought it was neat. But in all the years I had gone to school here, no one ever spoke up to stop Liam or anyone else from making fun of the "bindi" I couldn't take off. My cheeks burned and I blinked away some tears that were trying to spill. I opened my notebook as Mr. Crowe thanked Avantika and began to teach us about thesis-paper structure. Not even bothering to make my favorite cow drawing in the margins, I pushed my pencil hard into the paper as I took notes, feeling far less like a welcome ambassador and more like a total outcast.

chapter
TEN

The first two days of Diwali flew by with the same old, same old at school and at home. I could never keep track of what was supposed to happen on those days or even what they were called. To remember, I had to glance at the Kalnirnay and read the Marathi words really slowly. It was the vertical calendar on long paper that listed the million holidays in India from lots of different religions, and had cheesy ads for biscuits and fairness creams at the top. The only difference from normal days was that Aai would do longer pujas for the holidays and the house would fill with the earthy perfume of her all-natural, synthetic-fragrance-free sandalwood incense sticks during her prayers.

But the third day of Diwali was different. It was Lakshmi

Pujan, the biggest day of Diwali for us. I showered after school, like we had to before going to the temple or doing a puja at home. I got dressed in my swimming suit and warm-ups for practice. Then I began turning lights on all around the house to welcome the goddess Lakshmi into our home. I turned on the lights under the upper cabinets in the kitchen. Aai lit the oil lamps with long wicks she had made by rolling cotton out into worms, like when you played with clay.

"You're dressed like that for puja?" she asked softly, eye-ing my warm-up suit. Aai was wearing a gorgeous purple sari with gold embroidery. The padar, draped over her bare midriff and pinned onto the shoulder of her sari blouse, flashed magenta or gold, depending on how the light hit it.

I could tell she was sad. Her voice always got soft when she was sad.

"Back in India we wear our nicest clothes and gold jewelry for Diwali, and you're in your Halloween costume."

"It's not my costume," I said, turning on the chandelier lights in the formal dining room next to the kitchen. "I mean, it was. But today it's for swimming practice."

"In India you wouldn't have had swimming practice. Schools and classes are all closed for the holidays. And some of the biggest Hindi movies of the year open during Diwali."

"Well, we don't live in India. We live in Michigan. And it's just a normal day here. Remember?" I added, turning on the family room light.

"What do you think it is, Diwali?" asked Dad, entering the kitchen dressed in a pink kurta and white salwar.

"Hilarious, Dad," I said, trying not to smile. But it *was* kind of funny for him to say it on Diwali, when all the lights were on in the house on purpose.

"Let's start puja before your practice," said Aai as we all stood in front of the little temple on the kitchen counter. "Hurry, or we'll be late."

A piece of jewelry from each family member was put into a plate alongside silver coins with the goddess Lakshmi on them, and some dollar bills. Aai drew a swastik out of red kunku and water on the counter. As the prayer began, I watched the diva's flame flicker against the silver image of Lakshmi. I put some flowers from the Jungle before the gods and then did namaskar.

When it was all done, I gobbled down the prasad Aai had made, besan laadus. I definitely ate more than my share of the sweet chickpea-flour laadus, but, hey, prasad was food that was offered to God first and then eaten, considered blessed. And I figured I needed more blessings and luck than Aai and Dad. After all, they weren't the ones who had to go to school with Liam or swim with Aidy.

I drank some water out of the little silver vessel that Aai kept out for fancy occasions and glanced at the clock. "We have to go!" I said to Aai, grabbing my duffel bag from the hallway. "Change fast, please. I can't be late."

Aai looked at the clock. "There's no time. Come on." She grabbed her keys and purse, throwing her long, gray winter jacket over her sari.

"You can't go like that!" I said, turning to my dad with pleading eyes. At least his outfit looked more like normal American clothes than my mom's. If he kept his coat on, no one would even realize he was wearing a long pink tunic.

"I can't. I have to dictate some cases for work," Dad said. "It was a really busy day, and I had to leave early for Lakshmi Pujan."

"Let's go, Lekha. Now," said Aai, heading into the garage with the car keys.

I watched her purple sari swoosh around her legs below

her coat. Picturing all the looks and questions we would get at practice, I suddenly found myself wishing we did live in India.

❀ ❀

I managed to match the pace of my tryout time in the freestyle at swimming, clocking in at twenty-nine seconds. Maybe I got a power boost from all the delicious fried food I had been munching on at home this week, while Aai relaxed her "avoid fried foods" rule. Or maybe it was because I was doing whatever I could do to distract Aidy from asking me any more sari questions than she already had, making me feel like I was going deeper and deeper underwater with each one, until I was as different from her as an ocean creature.

"What's your mom wearing? Do you wear saris? Why not? Do you have to be a certain age to wear them? Does it feel weird to have your belly out in them all day? I thought you're not allowed to show any skin?"

I was grateful when we were finally no longer in viewing distance of Aai's sari in the locker room. I showered quickly and pulled my swim cap off my head, pulling some hair out in the process. I pinned my lock of curls back where it normally hung.

"Everyone swam so well today," said Harper loudly, blow-drying her hair.

"I feel like we're finally becoming a team good enough to beat Preston," said Aidy, referring to the Dolphins' arch-nemesis and neighboring town's swim club.

Harper nodded. "We should do a team dinner to celebrate!" she said over the noise.

"Let's go to Joe's!" Kendall added, pulling a sweater over her head. "Like we used to."

"That would be so fun," said Aidy as the blow-dryer finally stopped yelling. "We used to do team dinners there after meets."

"I'm in," said Harper. "I'm starving, too."

"Me too," said Kendall.

"Lekha?" asked Aidy.

I chewed at the inside of my cheek. I had to do this. I had to have a terrible conversation with Aai. I had to beg her to let me go to a restaurant on Diwali instead of eating with my family. It was either that or forever be the outcast on the team.

I took a shaky breath in. "I'll ask my mom." I zipped up my duffel bag, already certain what her answer would be. No matter how different today might have felt, it was still going to be same old, same old Aai. No holiday would change that.

chapter
ELEVEN

"You can't go," said Aai, jingling her car keys in her hand in the lobby of the Sports Club. Behind her, a TV on mute showed images of Winters and Sharpe debating. A few feet away, Kendall, Harper, Aidy, and their parents watched us talk, waiting by the glass doors to the parking lot. "Sorry."

I smiled at Aidy and turned back to Aai. "Please. It's a team-bonding thing. And Aidy's mom has a van. She can drive us all and drop me back home."

Aai shook her head and started speaking in Marathi. "Maajhi ani Aidy chya aai chi olakh nahi."

Hot. I felt hot all over my face as I saw everyone staring at the funny words coming out of Aai's mouth. I grabbed her elbow and walked a few steps farther away from the parents. "They can hear you," I whispered.

"I was talking in Marathi."

"Yeah. And they obviously know it's about them."

"So what? I'm not ashamed. And I'm not sending you with a driver I don't know."

"She's my teammate's mom. She gets her daughter to school and swimming safely, just like you. Please. I'll be fine. I'm not a baby anymore," I whispered, my voice oddly trembling, like I was a baby about to cry.

"It's Diwali."

I watched Aidy tap her foot impatiently as her mom aimed her key chain at the dark parking lot to start the heat in the car. "Please?"

Aai shook her head. "They wouldn't beg their parents to have dinner with friends away from their family on Christmas."

"It's different."

"*Kaay* different *aahe*?"

"Nothing stops for our holidays. There's no vacation from school for Diwali. It's just a regular day here, remember? This isn't India."

Aai shook her head, tucking her hair behind her ear as the gold bangles on her wrists jingled loudly and everyone looked our way. "I'm sorry, Lekha."

*   *

I didn't say much on the car ride home. Every time Aai turned the wheel and her bangles tapped against each other, I thought about my teammates and their parents all staring at us, and I felt hot and embarrassed all over again.

When we got home, Dad had heated up our dinner and had it waiting on the table for us.

"How did swimming go?" he asked.

I dropped my duffel bag to the ground in the hallway, not even caring that my stainless-steel water bottle probably got dented from the fall. "Fantastic," I grumbled, washing my hands.

Aai told dad in Marathi that I was mad that I didn't get to go to dinner with my friends.

Dad shook his head, pouring a spoonful of piping hot aamti, a different kind of lentil soup than varan, onto my bhaat. "Aai's right, Lekha. It's Diwali. Look at all this food she spent all day making." With the aamti soaking into my rice, he tapped a small silver spoon of toop over it, causing a little mound of the ghee to fall into the aamti bhaat volcano and melt like lava down the sides. "This is our holiday."

"And that's my team." I tore at my poli and scooped up the batata bhaji. I knew Aai had made it because the potato dish was one of my favorites. She had even browned the potato in oil, and given me all the crunchy burnt bits off the serving spoon. That was my favorite part of this bhaji. But I was too annoyed to thank her.

"And we're your family," Dad said, a little sterner than before.

"Fine. Whatever," I responded, thinking about all the fun my teammates were having without me. And all the pizza and garlic knots they would get to eat while I was stuck eating Indian food. I shoved bite after bite into my mouth as Aai and Dad discussed boring things like Dad's work and what our relatives in India were up to on Diwali.

Aaji went to a couple of classical singing concerts in Mumbai. One of my uncles was in charge of their apartment building's celebrations and hired a "mimicry artist" to come and impersonate all the Bollywood stars. Sheetal Mavshi, my mom's sister, was at the theater, trying to see two Hindi movies in one day. And in between eating tons of amazing Diwali food, my cousins organized protests against fireworks, which killed birds and caused pollution. My family in India was having a blast. My teammates were having a blast. And I was stuck at home with my parents. It was so unfair.

I downed my water, half listening as Aai talked about Diwali when she was a kid.

"We were so excited to take this train across India for a Diwali family reunion at my great-grandmother's house in Nagpur. We had been talking about it for months. All the cousins wrote one another letters, so excited for this get-together. . . . But then the train broke down and we were stuck in the middle of nowhere for hours. I was so hungry. A man who was sitting next to us had gotten on at the last stop. He said this happened all the time to this line, and it would be eight hours before it was fixed. At least. Can you believe that?"

"Nope," I said, barely listening. I stared at my distorted reflection in the stainless-steel plate that had the murky remains of aamti, bhaat, poli crumbs, and stray cumin seeds across it.

"The man, a total stranger, told my parents that Ajay Mama and I must have been hungry. Sheetal Mavshi wasn't born yet, but Ajay Mama was just two at the time. So you know what that man did? He got down, and this is before cell phones, Lekha. He got down, walked back to the last train station, called his home on a pay phone, and asked his wife to make us a meal. He took a taxi forty minutes home, packed the food into tiffins, and came back two hours later with dinner for the whole family."

Aai turned to me as I headed with my plate to the sink. "Now, that's India for you."

In no mood to join Aai on this trip down memory lane anymore while my social life was being derailed, I angrily let go of the plate. It clanged against the stainless-steel sink repeatedly, like booming thunder, before settling in silence.

"Lekha," Aai said sharply. "Upstairs. Now."

I stomped up the stairs, Aai right behind me. I could see the Christmas lights on my parents' bedroom curtain rods from the hall, even before we entered the room. Aai paused, distracted from whatever lecture she was about to give me.

"Doesn't it look beautiful?" she asked. "It's the magic of Diwali. If only you'd appreciate it."

I stared at the dresser, at the baby picture of me Aai kept right next to a faded black-and-white picture of her parents and Sheetal Mavshi smiling as Ajay Mama tilted his head back in what had to be the loud laugh he was known for.

"Hello?" Aai asked impatiently.

"I didn't hear you," I snapped, still annoyed with my mother.

"You need a good tel malish," she said, spreading an old paisley cotton sari of her mother's onto the carpet to protect it from grease stains. "Your head needs to cool down."

"I told you I'm not a baby anymore," I replied, sitting down across from the silver devghar on the dresser, where Aai did her pujas in the morning. "I can put coconut oil in my own hair."

I was hoping she would listen, or I would need my third shower of the day. I always put just the right amount of organic coconut oil into my hair to make my curls stay in place. I say "just the right amount" because Aai used to oil my hair so much that when I would walk to elementary school in winter, the oil that had turned clear in the heat of her palms would start to solidify. The chunks of cloudy white against my black curls were just one more thing for the fifth-grade boys to tease me about.

"It's not coconut oil," Aai replied. She went to her bathroom and emerged with the dreaded Mahabhringraj Tel.

It was an ayurvedic oil made out of herbs, kept in an amber-colored glass bottle. When Aai poured the olive-green oil onto her hands and put the oil on my scalp, my head would suddenly go cold, like peppermint was touching it. It smelled like bitter food and gas, like when Dad kept flicking the stove dial on but the range wouldn't light. The stink was so bad, I could swear my hair still smelled like it even after a washing. This was probably because Aai made me use an all-natural shampoo made from the Indian tree shikakai. It was ugly brown and lumpy, and nothing like the smooth, white, scented shampoos everyone else used.

"You know," Aai said, unscrewing the cap and letting the awful stench escape the bottle, "one of the things I will never forget about those two hours we were stuck in the dark on that train, before that man brought us food, was that we were all together."

I scrunched my nose and closed my eyes, frowning as the cool trickle of oil began to slither down my scalp. I couldn't help but relax as Aai worked her fingers into my skin. It felt calming, and for a brief instant I almost forgot why I was so mad. Almost.

"We were scared," Aai continued. "It was pitch-dark outside. Who knew what animals were out in the wilderness. Who knew what kind of people were out there, or what they could do to us. Ajay Mama was crying. We were all hungry. But Aaji and Ajoba started a game of Antakshari with us."

Antakshari was a singing game where one person would sing a few lines of a song, and the next person would have to sing a song that started with the letter the previous person ended with. People in India loved to play it at weddings, on long road trips, on vacations, and I guess even on a broken train in the middle of nowhere.

"Soon we were all singing old Hindi songs and laughing together in the dark, cold train, ignoring the howling animals and hooting birds outside. In that moment we were all together on Diwali, safe, and that was all that mattered. And that's how I like us to be every Diwali." Aai massaged the oil into my skin and the roots of my hair. "I lost my father when you were a baby, Sheetal Mavshi and Aaji are in India, and Ajay Mama is in California. But you, Dad, and I are here, so shouldn't we be together on Diwali?" Aai asked, softly.

I shrugged.

"I know. It's been a long day. You're tired. I know you wanted to go with your team. But Diwali is not a day to leave your family. It's a day to be with your family. To make memories. I know you think I'm just mean, but everything I do is to protect you, to help you. . . . Next time I'll think about it, and if the circumstances are right, I'll let you go."

I opened my eyes. "You will?"

"If the circumstances are right, yes." Aai got up to wash her hands and put away the oil. She opened her dresser drawer. "That means not on a holiday, among other things."

I watched her pull out a small blue gift bag I had seen for years. It was made out of an old Indian outfit of mine that had torn, and Aai used it to give me a present every Diwali.

"Happy Diwali," Aai said, handing me the bag.

"What about Dad? He'll probably want to take pictures."

"Why take pictures? It's just a regular day, right? No big deal?"

I rubbed my thumb on the twisted handles of the bag, made out of my old shoulder straps. "Sorry," I mumbled.

Aai smiled. She called out to my dad and asked him to hurry with the camera.

As Dad clicked away and Aai just watched with shiny eyes, I reached inside the bag and pulled out an animal joke book. I flipped through it. There were animal knock-knock jokes, animal riddles, and even an entire chapter on animal puns I *gnu* would make Noah miserable.

"Thanks," I mumbled again, even softer than my apology.

Aai did her best grumpy Lekha impression. "I didn't hear you."

"Thanks," I said, a little louder, trying not to smile.

"Suhana safar aur yeh mausam haseen." Aai sang the old Hindi movie song as she sat next to me, grinning for a picture. *"Hame dar hai ham kho na jaaye kahi."*

"Huh!" said Dad, putting his camera on the dresser and sitting in front of me, never one to turn down a game of Antakshari. "Uh . . . *Hum aapke hain kaun!*"

"Nuh." Aai pointed to me, assigning me my Hindi letter.

"Nuh way am I doing this," I said with a little smile.

Aai started to sing on my behalf, Dad joined her, singing the girl's part way out of his range, and soon we were all laughing. The flickering divas and window lights danced all around me and my family as we hung out together on Diwali.

chapter
TWELVE

*A*ll the warm and fuzzy feelings from Lakshmi Pujan started to turn cold when Aidy and Harper walked into the PE locker room the next day in tears.

I glanced at Avantika, who was tying her shoes, now a pro at changing in public.

"What's wrong?" I asked.

Aidy snorted as she shoved her clothes into her locker, and I quickly realized they were tears of joy, from laughing too hard.

"Breadstick Boy is what's wrong," Harper giggled, changing into her gym clothes.

Aidy doubled over laughing as they headed out the door.

Avantika was still busy with her shoelaces, so I quickly

followed my teammates to the gym. Most of the class was already seated on the shiny wooden floor. Mr. Jennings had taped off large squares, divided into quarters around the room.

"Come on, girls!" he shouted. "Hustle, hustle, hustle."

Aidy and Harper took a seat in the back row of our class. I plopped down next to them as Avantika walked out, heading our way.

"Who is Breadstick Boy?" I asked.

"Oh my God. Stop," said Aidy, looking at Harper as she began to crack up again. "You're going to get us in trouble. PS: What's that smell?" she asked, sniffing in my direction.

I tucked a curl behind my ear, wishing I hadn't heard that question, because I knew the answer. It was the curse of the Mahabhringraj Tel. Despite washing my hair again at night, I was haunted by its musty scent. I wanted to tell Aidy to drop it, to tell her that it was an oil made with herbs from an ancient Indian form of medicine, that my kind of hair was different from hers and needed the oil, but instead, I just desperately searched for a topic to change the subject to so I wouldn't have to hear the question again.

"You really should have come out with us last night,"

Harper whispered, saving me, as Avantika sat down next to me.

"Yeah. You missed out," agreed Aidy.

Mr. Jennings blew his whistle loudly. "All right. Eyes on me, everyone." He pointed to the square. "Today it's Flashback Friday. So we're going to play a game from when I was a kid."

"One hundred years ago?" asked a kid from the front.

Everyone started to laugh. Mr. Jennings grinned. "Funny guy. And close. It's called four square. You're going to break up into groups of four. One kid will stand in each square. The person who starts has to pass the ball to a teammate. It has to bounce once, and then the next person has to catch it before it bounces again. Then they throw it to someone else, the same way. If it bounces more than once before you catch it, you're out. And if you miss it, you're out. Got it?"

We all nodded.

"Great. Let's go. You four, you're a team," Mr. Jennings said, pointing at the back to me, Avantika, Harper, and Aidy. "Next four, you're a team. . . ."

Mr. Jennings's voice trailed off as Avantika and I followed Harper and Aidy to the large square in the far corner of the gym. Avantika picked up the big brown rubber ball, and we each took a spot in one of the four squares inside the large square.

"Everyone ready?"

We nodded. She bounced the ball once and Aidy easily caught it. Aidy bounced the ball to Harper, who caught it and bounced it to Avantika, forgetting about me. Avantika bounced the ball my way.

"Was the food good?" I asked, bouncing the bumpy ball at Harper.

Harper nodded, catching it. "So good." She bounced the ball to Aidy.

"Except for the breadsticks," Aidy squeaked, trying not to laugh as she bounced the ball to Harper.

Harper started to laugh and missed the ball.

"You're out!" Aidy exclaimed.

"So not fair! You distracted me with—"

"With Breadstick Boy," I muttered, picking up the ball and reminding myself that School Lekha keeps her mouth shut when things bug her. I threw the ball to Avantika.

"Who is Breadstick Boy?" she asked, examining my face, which was twisting with frustration and rejection.

"It's just this kid who was eating at the table across from us," replied Aidy. "He was cracking us up with the way he was eating breadsticks." Aidy caught the ball and threw it back to Avantika. "You had to be there."

"Yeah," said Harper as Avantika bounced the ball back to Aidy.

Aidy missed. "I'm out too," she said, hopping over to Harper.

"Next time you have to come with us, Lekha. You can't miss team bonding," added Harper as Avantika and I began to bounce the ball back and forth to each other.

"I didn't want to miss it. My mom wouldn't let me go," I replied, throwing the ball back harder to Avantika.

She gave me a small frown, catching it and bouncing it back before turning to Harper and Aidy. "Of course she missed it. It's Diwali."

Aidy's eyes widened as she grabbed Harper's arm. "See? I told you guys it had to be some Indian thing." Aidy looked at me. "I felt bad for you, missing out on all the fun."

"Me too," said Harper.

"Not as bad as I felt for Breadstick Boy's mom, though," said Aidy, grinning.

Harper snickered. "I can't believe I almost forgot about that. Remember her face when he did the walrus thing?"

Aidy's and Harper's giggles bounced off the gym walls, and I swatted the ball to the ground. It went diagonal, and Avantika missed it.

"I'm out," she said, stepping next to Harper and Aidy. They were too busy giggling and pretending they were eating breadsticks in their annoying little inside joke to notice.

I watched as the ball stopped bouncing and rolled around lifelessly on the floor, as if it had given up. Even though everyone else was out, I couldn't help but feel like I was the loser.

chapter THIRTEEN

𝒪n Saturday, the last day of Diwali, called Bhaubeej, I sat on the porch, reading with Noah. Cookie, who was bundled up in a crocheted yellow-and-black-striped bumblebee sweater Noah's dad had made for her, sat beside us.

Bhaubeej was the day brothers gave their sisters gifts. Since I was an only child, my cousins in India would send me Amar Chitra Kathas each year. They were comic books filled with Indian mythology, history, and stories from different religions, and I loved to read them. Noah was finishing up one about a monkey outwitting a crocodile, while I read one about the Marathi emperor Shivaji. It was cold, and we had to go to Detroit for Diwali festivities, but I knew we'd have a few more minutes to wait because Aai was on the phone with Ajay Mama. Her brother in Berkeley always called on Bhaubeej, and they would chat for at least an hour.

"This is almost as good as *Musings*," said Noah, talking about his favorite magazine.

I nodded. The Halloween ghost that once guarded the porch had now been replaced by solar-powered strings of Diwali lights, and they twinkled above us. Under the lights, I squeezed my peacoat closed over my sleeveless salwar kurta.

The kurta was a maroon tunic with shiny, embroidered gold flowers that went to my knees. The teal salwar ballooned out at the thighs, like harem pants. I had a teal odhani with glistening gold sequins around my neck. Although my birth-mark was still covered by my hair, a real, sparkling maroon and gold bindi was on my forehead. I had matching maroon, teal, and gold bangles on too, and loved the way they seemed to sing whenever I moved my hands to pet Cookie.

I looked across the street at Avantika's house and wondered what she would be wearing to the temple. I had no clue what Maya and Tanvi, my family friends from Detroit, would think of her. Would we even be able to talk about the stuff we normally talked about, or would our conversation be super polite and boring, the way we had to act in front of relatives in India when we met them for the first time?

I tried not to think about it as we watched Mr. Giordano rake his grass and accidentally scratch the wire feet of his WINTERS FOR CONGRESS sign. It jolted like it had been electrocuted. He had a new blue sign with white letters near his porch too, which said, DON'T LIKE IT?

I didn't know why, but something about the sign, something about that question, made my stomach drop.

Noah saw me staring at it and rolled his eyes. "Winters's new slogan. It's what she says at her rallies. 'Don't like it? Leave.' My parents say she's the worst."

"Looks like a lot of people think she's the best." I pointed down the street, trying to shake the nervous feeling. Behind the row of almost bare trees that lined the curb, four more houses had the distinctive blue sign with white letters that asked, DON'T LIKE IT?

"I think my op-ed is going to be about how un-American it is to say things like that," Noah said, flipping a crunchy brown maple leaf that had blown our way in between his palms by rubbing its stem back and forth. "Like, no one has a right to say someone doesn't deserve to be here, you know?"

I shrugged. This was not something I wanted to think about. "I have no clue what mine is going to be about."

Across the street, Avantika's car pulled out of her driveway. Her whole family waved to us as they zoomed down the street.

"I really don't feel strongly about anything," I said, ignoring the little bit of fear that was trying to crawl into my brain. I threw a pine cone back into the bed of the three large white pines that loomed over our front yard.

"That's not true," Noah said over the grumbling of our garage door as it opened for Dad to pull his shiny Ford Taurus out.

Finally done with her call, Aai was seated inside, in her gold sari with the shimmering purple and green border.

I quickly stood up, petting Cookie good-bye on the head, and gave Noah my comic to borrow. "I have to 'Don't like it, *leave.*'" I grinned.

But Noah tried not to smile. "It's not funny. It's serious. It's un-American."

I waved as I got into the car. I had bigger things to worry about than Abigail Winters. I had just one hour to figure out how to make my childhood friends, whom I saw only a few times a year, fine with hanging out with Avantika.

The November chill made my toes, in my gold, sequined chappal, feel like carrots straight out of the fridge, so I ran up the marble steps of the Hindu Temple. I headed past the two giant elephant statues that seemed to guard the entrance, and entered the building.

The smell of sandalwood incense and rose water swirled in the air as we took our shoes off in the room to the left. We placed them in cubbies near each other to make leaving easier and hung up our coats, the metal hangers sounding like the percussion section of our middle school band as they clanged against one another. Groups of teenagers were hanging out in the coatroom, some half hidden behind the heavy winter jackets, giggling and snickering to one another as they chatted or read something on a cell phone. They were the "big kids," and we never said much to each other, other than "Hey."

I nodded a few greetings to the various cliques and started to head for the stairs to find my friends in the cafeteria downstairs, but Dad motioned toward the main temple doors. "Namaskar first," he reminded me.

A large white man was standing in front of the doors in a

navy-blue uniform with an embroidered patch on his shoulder that said, GREAT LAKES SECURITY.

Aai squeezed Dad's elbow. "Why is there a guard here?" she asked as the cold marble tiles below our feet changed to thin, gray, looped Berber carpet in the hall.

Avantika's dad was inside, near the prasad table, talking to some other uncles and aunties, dressed in their Diwali best. He waved to us as we neared. "They were just telling me that the donation box was stolen earlier this week. What a shame."

I looked at the west side of the hall, where the rows of marble deities wearing vibrantly colored saris, fashioned into dhotis and sashes for the gods and little saris for the goddesses, stood. Right in front of them, the metal donation box with an intricately carved floral pattern was missing. Instead, there was now just a small wooden chest with a slit in the top for sliding dollar bills into after praying, to help maintain the temple.

Near it was Deepika Auntie and Avantika. Avantika was dressed in a mango-orange Anarkali-style kurta that went down to her ankles. She had on a tight yellow chudidar salwar that bunched at her ankles and a sunny-yellow odhani. I watched as they walked from idol to idol. They paused before each one to crouch on their knees, their palms together in a namaskar at their forehead, and bow down until their heads touched the ground. I kept eyeing Avantika's salwar-kurta. It was probably brand-new from India, in the latest style, which was a long kurta.

My own salwar-kurta was a hand-me-down from Ajay Mama's friends in California. It was old and out of fashion. Styles changed quickly in Indian clothes. A few years ago harem pants like I had on were in. Now tight pants and leggings were. Back then everyone wore short tops like mine, but now everyone was wearing ankle-length tops, including some old aunties walking by me in the temple.

I cringed. Aunties were dressed better than me. Trying not to think about my fashion disaster, I ran forward, my eyes locked on one thing: the brass bell that hung from the ceiling. I jumped up and hit it a few times, letting the peaceful reverberations fill the temple. Avantika turned to me, a small smile on her face, but Aai narrowed her eyes until her tikli looked like it was going to fall off from the wrinkles forming on her forehead. It was her "subtle" reminder to me to not overdo the bell and disturb others.

Dad joined us and we did our namaskars, put a few dollars into the wooden box, and then ate some prasad. Today the temple had my favorite in a bowl next to the bananas and apples. It was badam, bedane, and khadi-sakhar. Dad scooped a spoonful into my right hand. I popped the almonds, raisins, and small, flat squares of opaque sugar into my mouth and, Avantika by my side, grabbed my chappal and headed downstairs.

"It smells so good," said Avantika as we took our plates and went through the buffet line, loading up with puris, fried golden rounds of bread that glistened with oil. I scooped some shrikhand, thick-strained yogurt sweetened with sugar and spiced with cardamom and saffron, crocus-flower stigmas that just happened to be the most expensive spice in the world. I added batata bhaji onto the side of my plate, eyeing the turmeric-stained cubes of boiled and panfried potatoes peppered with mustard seeds and curry leaves. I scooched my bhaji over to make room for the varan bhaat, and added a bigger helping than was polite of the spicy, tangy mango pickle.

"My friends are at the table at the end," I told Avantika. I normally would have run to them squealing because we hadn't seen each other in so long. But today I felt like I was about to ruin the fun, or like I had to act differently in front of Avantika. We walked toward Maya and Tanvi, who were at the end of a long table crowded with all the kids whose names I couldn't remember, since we barely came to town anymore.

Maya, dressed in a long, sleeveless, dark-green Anarkali that went down to her ankles, highlighted by a magenta, purple, and gold odhani, was picking at her varan bhaat with her spoon, making a face. Tanvi's Anarkali was mustard yellow with navy-blue embroidery all over it, except on her long sleeves, which were sheer gold with a floral pattern on them. Done with her food, she was twisting her blue odhani around her arm like a snake and undoing it, over and over again.

I tugged at the bottom of my kurta with my free hand, wishing it would magically grow past my thighs, and took a seat. "Hey, guys. This is Avantika. Avantika, this is Maya and Tanvi. We've been friends, like, since we were born."

"Hi, everyone," Avantika said, and smiled, pulling a chair from the table behind us.

"Are you the cousin from Pune?" asked Maya, putting her spoon down as she gave up on the varan bhaat.

Avantika looked confused, so I quickly spoke up. "We're not cousins. We're neighbors."

"What? You moved to Oakridge? From India?"

"Why?" asked Tanvi, throwing her odhani back over her neck. "There's nothing there." She turned red as she looked at me. "I mean, of course, there is stuff there. I didn't mean—"

"It's fine." I shrugged, pushing my bindi to make sure it was still sticking in place. "There's definitely not as much stuff to do there as there is here." I paused, annoyed at myself for putting down my hometown so easily in front of my friends. Oakridge had its flaws, but I loved my house. I loved living next door to Noah. I loved how pretty our downtown looked year-round, whether it was blooming with tulips in spring, swirled with red, white, and blue ribbons for the Fourth of July, decorated with skeletons in poses from famous movies in October, or twinkling with Christmas lights at the end of the year.

"I love your salwar-kurta," said Maya to Avantika. "Very cool. You must really miss the shopping back home."

Maya's words were starting to take on a very slight Indian accent. It was something I subconsciously did in India, too, when talking to my aunts and uncles, so they could understand my thick American accent better.

Before Avantika could answer, Tanvi snorted. "Why are you talking like a fob, Maya?"

Maya swatted the air near Tanvi with her odhani, giggling. "I'm so not! If I was talking like a fob, I'd be like, 'I luvv your salwar-kurrrta. Verry cool.'"

Tanvi laughed. "See? I told you, fob."

I started to smile but saw Avantika quickly spoon a glob of shrikhand into her mouth, a flush of red spreading over her cheeks.

I sighed as Tanvi and Maya cluelessly continued their impressions, remembering what Dad had said about what it felt like to be made fun of just for being who you are. I knew that feeling well. And it was a horrible feeling. "Your parents are fobs," I said hesitantly, over their laughter.

They stopped. I froze too, a little shocked at the words that had slipped out.

"They are not. Not anymore, anyway. Their accents aren't that bad," said Tanvi.

"Shah Rukh Khan is a fob." I frowned, mentioning Maya's favorite Bollywood actor.

"He is not. He doesn't live here so he isn't fresh off any

boat, and— Oh." Maya seemed to turn a little green when she saw Avantika's flushed face. "We didn't mean it. I wasn't even thinking."

Avantika kept looking down, and I thought I saw a tear plop onto her plate.

"It was just a joke," said Tanvi, scooting her chair back with a screech. "Anyway, I'm stuffed. We'll meet you guys at the coatracks, okay?" she added, grabbing Maya's arm.

"Sorry," I said softly, wishing I had put a stop to the joke earlier.

Avantika stuffed a big bite of puri with batata bhaji in her mouth so she could only nod.

"Next time we'll get here earlier so their mouths are stuffed like yours. Then they can't make so many awful jokes."

Avantika nodded again.

"And, hey, maybe you could pack some batata bhaji for Liam, too. I could use some silence from him."

Avantika smiled. "He'd probably get grossed out by the name and think it's made out of butts or something."

I laughed, chewing on the mango pickle until it got so hot, I needed to swallow it and chug some water. "'Mr. Crowe!

Dot and Dot are eating butts! Is that allowed in America?'"

"'Ew, Dot! Why does it look like that?'" said Avantika, doing her best American accent. "'Why does it smell?'"

I sat backward in my chair like Mr. Crowe, easily done thanks to my ugly, short kurta. "'Because it's butts, Liam.'"

And with that, I started laughing so hard, I could barely speak. Avantika was cracking up, happy tears washing away whatever tears were there before.

"Do you want to have a sleepover?" I blurted.

Avantika paused. "Sure. I've never had one back home."

I tried to sound like a seasoned sleepover expert. "We just watch movies, and pig out, and go to sleep."

Avantika nodded. "That sounds like fun. And if you want to do it at my house, we can pig out on bhel. Your favorite."

"As long as your mom remembers to put batata in it." I grinned.

chapter

FOURTEEN

The bhel at Avantika's was amazing. Auntie had loaded the puffed rice with potatoes, raw mango, onions, tomatoes, fried strings of shev, small chickpeas, cilantro chutney (which I was okay with, even though I normally couldn't stand cilantro), and my favorite, tangy, sweet, chincha chutney. I had eaten three large bowls of the bhel, and at the end, when I saw Avantika open a cabinet and pop a few brown hamster-turds in her mouth, I begged her to let me have some too.

They weren't really rodent doo-doos. They just looked like them. And probably had a similar sulfuric stink. They were chewable ayurvedic herb tablets that helped you digest your food and cured stomachaches. "Delicious digestives," as their commercial jingle went. We had run out of ours in summer and hadn't had a chance to go to the Indian store in Detroit to restock our supply before Diwali at the temple. They had a strong, farty odor, yet strangely tasted delicious, but they were definitely not something you'd eat with your friends because, well, who wants to smell like farts? But I felt comfortable with Avantika, and figured if we both ate them, it wouldn't matter who "smelt it."

With our meal finished, Avantika and I said good night to her parents and headed up to her room. My plaid, blue, flame-retardant-free, organic-cotton sleeping bag, purchased by Aai (of course) after months of searching, was already laid out on the floor, smooth and crisp. She had taken forever finding a sleeping bag that was free of toxins a few years back. I was so annoyed, thinking of all the sleepovers I was missing out on while she wasted time reading blog after blog about what could harm your sleeping child. But in the end, it came, and the only people who even got to use it were my little cousins from California, who took turns sleeping in it when they came to visit.

I reached into the sleeping bag's zippered pocket and pulled out my last Halloween candy bar. I made sure to hand it over before my hand heat-ray destroyed it.

"What's that?" Avantika asked.

"A little bit of Halloween, since you missed out on it."

Avantika smiled, eating her chocolate bar as I flipped through some *Archie Double Digest*s, the comics all my cousins in India had. I had some of my parents' Archies from when they were kids back home in my bookcase. So much of what was in Avantika's house reminded me of my house.

When I brushed my teeth, I saw the familiar yellow cylindrical container of Vicco Tooth Powder, the dark brown herb powder that Aai would have me put on my teeth every now and then with my finger to strengthen my gums and teeth. Next to it was a little jar of sea salt just like the one we kept in our bathroom drawer. I rubbed it on my gums at home once a month, and after rinsing it out, always hoped to find a little grain of salt left to suck on. And in front of the salt was this ayurvedic eye medicine for when your eyes felt tired. If anyone else saw it, they'd think I was joking when I said you took the medicine, which looked like honey, and rubbed it on your lower eyelid, right where your lashes were, and then it burned like fire and you cried and could finally wash it out. Everything was familiar, even if it wasn't the exact same. Instead of a framed, painted image of Ganpati on her walls like I had, she had a wooden Ganpati statue on her desk, next to her computer. Instead of Aamir Khan posters, she had Shah Rukh Khan posters.

I looked out Avantika's blinds at the houses down the street, and I couldn't help but wonder what Noah was up to tonight. It felt strange being at a sleepover on our street and not hanging out with him, but he had made his sleepover-less bed. Now he had to lie in it.

"So . . . I Googled sleepovers before you came," said Avantika, sitting awkwardly at her desk. "And we're supposed to watch movies . . . and do each other's hair?"

I laughed, flipping through all of Avantika's beautiful Indian clothes hanging in her closet. "You Googled it?"

Avantika fiddled with her computer screen. "Well, I've never hosted an American sleepover before."

"I'm sure it's not that different from a sleepover in India," I said, acting like a sleepover pro. "But let's skip the doing each other's hair thing. My hair's not like yours. I actually have to put it in a bunch of braids each night or I wake up with a giant knot. And on the weekends I have to put coconut oil in the braids overnight before I wash it, or it gets all dried out."

Avantika turned toward me. "You can do that here. I don't mind. I oil my hair every night."

I shook my head, my heavy bun swinging so hard, it weighed my neck down.

"Why? You can only have that one hairstyle in public?"

"If I don't want to get called Dot at school, yes," I replied, pulling the bobby pin out and swiping my frizzy curls off my forehead so my nosy neighbor could see the freckle above my eyebrows in the dead center of my forehead.

"Wow. So lucky!"

"Lucky?"

"You have a natural bindi. A birthmark? It's good luck."

"Not in Oakridge."

"Why do you cover up everything that makes you *you*? So what if people know you like samosas or Bollywood? Or if they know you're Indian?"

"I'm American," I said, quickly pinning my hair back in place. "Anyway, you don't know what it's like growing up here. Feeling different."

Avantika shrugged, removing her seashell clip so her silky hair fell like rippling ocean waves by her face. "I'm pretty different and I don't feel embarrassed. I heard someone laughing in math about my hair clip, but I don't care. It reminds me of the sea. It reminds me of home. So who cares?"

"I would. I can't even handle looks from Indian people at the temple when I'm in some hideous old outfit," I responded, thinking about how confident Avantika was compared to me.

"Your salwar-kurta was beautiful. Now how about we start the movie? It's really full of hideous old outfits, but I think you're going to like it anyway, Manju." She smiled, turning the large monitor on her desk so it faced her bed.

Aai would never let me have a computer in my room. She was worried about radiation. I was the only kid who had to keep my tablet on my desk instead of on my lap at school, like a baby being protected from everything. And I was one of the handful who didn't have a cell phone. I supposed it was for the best, given how many times Aai lectured Dad when she caught him coming home from work with his cell phone in his pocket instead of in his work bag.

I got into my sleeping bag and Avantika got under her covers as *ChaalBaaz* began to play on the screen, and we watched Sridevi dance in her peak 1989 fashion. I happily munched on the microwaved popcorn Avantika's dad had made us, enjoying the nuked kernels. Aai only let us eat popcorn made in a giant pot on the stove in slow motion, using our microwave as a giant clock instead of something to cook with.

We cracked up at Manju's, the rebellious twin's, antics. We rolled our eyes at Anju, the scaredy-cat twin. And we cheered when they switched places and totally confused their friends and family members.

"I think you need to find your inner Manju," said Avantika from the bed, putting face cream on as she watched Manju beat up the bad guys. "Want some?" She tossed me the tube.

"This is Fair & Dainty," I said, looking at the light-skinned model on the tube. There was no way I was going to use it. "It bleaches your skin. Doesn't it burn? I remember my aunt made me use it once in India, and my whole face turned red and it burned. And then Aai found out and they got into a huge fight and didn't speak for the rest of our trip."

Avantika looked down. "My mom wants me to use it. We both use it every night."

"Why?" I asked, even though I knew the answer. So many Indians were obsessed with light skin. They thought you were beautiful only if you were fair. Like it made you a better person or something. My aunt got the cream for me because she thought she was helping me, since I was the darkest person in my family. And the last time I was in an Indian store in Detroit, I was shocked to see tons more skin-lightening creams from American companies there, too, which they would never sell at an American store.

"You don't know what it's like, feeling different because of the color of your skin."

Was she serious? Did she have any clue just how white Oakridge was? And how not white I was? And wasn't she supposed to be the confident one out of the two of us?

"There arc ads all the time in India about being fair. In the paper. On TV. It's the first thing my relatives comment on when they see me after a long time."

"I've seen the ads. And they are so unbelievable, they're hilarious. Have you seen the one where the girl wants to break barriers and become a cricket announcer? But she's dark so she doesn't get the job? And then she puts the cream on and lightens up and suddenly they want her on TV?"

Avantika nodded.

"That one was playing in every commercial break the last time I was in India."

"It's not just Fair & Dainty. There's also Fair & Macho. It's for men."

I laughed, trying to force a popcorn kernel out from between my back teeth with my tongue. "Come on. You have to hear how funny this all sounds."

Avantika smiled. "There was a light bulb ad once where a girl kept getting passed on for arranged marriages because the grooms' families thought she was dark. But then they got the new light bulbs and everything was bright and she was actually fair skinned under that light, and a family seeing her immediately said yes."

"Okay. So then you have to toss that cream. Save yourself some burning face."

Avantika hesitantly took the tube from me.

"Come on. Chuck it."

Avantika went over to the trash can under her computer and tossed the tube in. But before I could even give her a "yay," she quickly fished it out.

"I'll just keep it in a drawer. In case my mom wants it back."

I nodded as Avantika turned the volume louder on the screen and we watched the twins work together to save the day. I snuck a glance over at Avantika, who was absent-mindedly rubbing at her cheeks, which were most probably stinging from the racist cream. I guessed I wasn't the only one who needed an inner Manju.

FIFTEEN

Thanksgiving at Maya's house was chaotic. But we were used to it. Since most of the people we knew in Detroit had family in other states and India, Desi Thanksgiving usually meant dinner with family friends. Tons of family friends. With a dozen families crammed into Maya's home, there was lots of noise, but lots of fun, too.

I sat at a small folding table in the sprawling walk-out basement with Maya and Tanvi, pulling my legs out of the way whenever a little kid went running by, zipping around the tables that separated people by age. The parents were in the middle, at the tables lining the wooden dance floor. Tiny kids and teenagers had their own areas. And there was one round table where Maya's grandparents, a bunch of their friends, and a couple of frail old grandmothers visiting from India sat.

We feasted on the traditional Thanksgiving meal of aamti, bhaat, poli, and lots of bhajis for the grown-ups, and salad, garlic bread, and vegetable lasagna stuffed with kidney beans for the kids. The only thing close to what Noah ate on Thanksgiving was the organic cranberries in a large bowl near the Indian food. I had heaped them on my plate, but they didn't go with my food. It was Aai's cranberry lonche, made by pickling the sliced cranberries with oil and mango pickle spices.

I guess we really were American-Born Confused Desis.

While Hindi music played over the speakers behind me, I looked at the huge framed pictures of Maya and her brother on the walls. The one closest to us was a picture of Maya doing raas at a national folk-dance competition in New York. She was an awesome dancer and could even do a twelve-step version of the raas. I finished my last bite of lasagna, thinking how Noah would have loved learning that raas from Maya.

"When are we playing charades?" asked Tanvi, swatting her hands together to get the garlic bread crumbs off.

"My brother is writing clues down," answered Maya. She

stopped picking at her lasagna to gesture toward the back of the basement, where the teenagers were giggling as they scribbled down embarrassing things for us to act out on little slips of paper.

Maya's ajoba passed us as he went to throw his plate in the trash. Maya wasn't exactly like me. Her parents were born here.

"Enjoying Thanksgiving?" he asked, his gray eyes getting more and more creases around them as he gave us a small smile.

"Yeah, Ajoba," I answered. I was always a little jealous of Maya for still having her grandfather, since both of mine had died before I even got to meet them. Maya's ajoba had immigrated to Missouri years ago for grad school before moving here to work at Ford, like lots of older Desis in Detroit.

"Lucky kids," he said, sitting next to us. "You know, when I first came here in 1967, I arrived on Thanksgiving, with just a suitcase, on my college campus. I didn't even have a place to stay."

I thought of Avantika. I wondered what her first day in Oakridge was like, before we met Halloween night, as Maya's grandfather continued.

"So, I knocked on the first door I saw. You know what the man said to me?"

"We know, Ajoba," said Maya. "No Indians . . . ," she started, and then looked down.

"No Indians, no Chinese, no dogs," Maya's grandfather finished. "And he slammed the door in my face."

I scratched my plastic fork against my paper plate, uncomfortably drawing lines into it as he continued. This must have been how Noah felt whenever I made a comment about skin color.

"I'll never forget that Thanksgiving. It was one of the hardest days of my life. I wanted to give up everything I had worked for. I wanted to forget about getting a PhD. I wanted to go home. But then, with each Thanksgiving that came, I got to see our families grow. And I got to see all of you. And I'm so glad I stayed and didn't give up. Because now this is home." He laughed. "When I go to India, it's so hot and uncomfortable for me now."

Maya grinned as fast Bollywood music began to play from the built-in speakers above us. "Yeah. We remember. You went from complaining about how the cold made your knees hurt here to complaining about the sun the last time we were in India. I'm pretty sure you complained the whole trip."

"Well, where do you think you get your complaining genes from?" Maya's grandfather pointed to the kidney beans she had picked out of the lasagna. "Let me guess, too dry? Too brown?"

"Too rajma," Maya replied, using the Hindi word for kidney beans.

Maya, her ajoba, and Tanvi all laughed. I smiled but was unable to shake the sad feeling I was getting after Ajoba's story. I couldn't help but wonder what Noah or Avantika would have said if they had been here to hear it. Actually, I knew what Noah would have said. He would have said it was a racist injustice and Ajoba should have written letters to the newspaper about it or tipped off a reporter so they'd cover the story.

Ajoba patted us all on the head and headed to the dessert table, which was covered with all sorts of pies and a casserole dish full of gaajar halwa, shredded carrots cooked in milk, sugar, and spices.

"Ooh, my song is on!" exclaimed Maya, pointing to the speaker. "Come on, I'll teach you my dance," she said.

"It's easy. She taught me right before you got here," added Tanvi, grabbing our plates and tossing them in the trash.

"Your dance for what?" I asked, standing up, dreading having to clumsily dance next to Maya and Tanvi for everyone to see.

"For their IASA show. It was yesterday," added Tanvi. "You're so lucky, Maya. Our middle school only has, like, forty Indian kids, so no IASA."

"What's an IASA?" I asked, following my friends around the tables full of people.

"Indian American Student Association," Maya replied, twisting her hand high above her as she began to gracefully shake her hips to the beat. "We just have thirty Indian kids in sixth grade, but there are about a hundred twenty in our IASA, with seventh and eighth grades and all the non-Desi kids, too."

I stopped just shy of the wooden floor, digging my socks into the thick, fluffy carpet surrounding it. I couldn't believe it. Maya's life must have been so different. Did she take Indian food to school for lunch, and did people actually ask what smelled good instead of what stank? Did people ask where her bindi was because they wanted to wear one too? Were the questions I got every day totally different from the ones Maya, or even Tanvi, heard?

It wasn't fair that my middle school experience was so different. That I was treated like an outsider. That Tanvi was bummed her school had "only" thirty-nine other kids who knew what she was going through, who knew her holidays, who knew her traditions. I frowned, tugging at my sweater sleeve, but Maya pulled me onto the dance floor. "Hop to the side here and follow us, okay?"

I clumsily stepped over my friends' feet and slid forward onto the wooden floor, watching as Tanvi followed Maya's lead, easily hopping to the dance she had just learned, alternating feet so quickly, I couldn't tell what she was doing. I laughed nervously and stepped side to side like a graceless, uncoordinated version of my friends.

Maya and Tanvi bent forward near me, pulsing their hands to the floor and up, spinning and crouching, coiling their arms.

"Come on," Tanvi said, lifting my arms as I just stood there.

Tanvi's mom let out the loud whistle she was known for

at all dancing events. Aai clapped at her table. M
had his cell phone out to record us. The teenag   ~~~~
cheering. And I was sweating.

"You can do it, Lekha," said Maya as she and Tanvi
twirled around me.

But I was frozen in place, a crooked, awkward smile on
my face. I wanted to tell Maya I wasn't comfortable dancing
in front of everyone. That I couldn't dance like her. That it
made me feel really bad about myself. I wanted to ask Tanvi
to stop moving my limbs like I was her puppet. That it was
making me look even worse than I felt. I opened my mouth to
speak, but the music was so thunderous, I heard the drums
beating in my chest louder than any voice I could muster.

"Did you say something?" Maya asked, huffing as the
song got faster.

I wish. There was so much I wanted to say to spare
myself this humiliation and stop it from happening again.
But instead, I just shook my head and changed the subject.
"I have to go to the bathroom. I'll be back." I retreated off
the dance floor, gave our audience an embarrassed wave,
and rushed through the maze of tables, around the stairwell,
to the safety of the bathroom.

I shut the door behind me, muting the thumping music that I would have had no problem dancing to in my room but couldn't stand hearing here. It was strange. It was the first time I could remember that I missed Oakridge while in Detroit.

chapter
SIXTEEN

I didn't have to miss Oakridge or my friends for too long. The Monday after Thanksgiving, Noah, Avantika, and I were back together again.

"You should have come to Maya's," I said to Avantika as she walked down her driveway to join Noah and me on the street. "You would've had fun." And I bet she would have seen how uncomfortable I was on the dance floor, said something, and given me company around the dessert table instead of forcing me to make a fool of myself in front of everyone.

Avantika shrugged, hiding her hands in her pockets. "I didn't grow up with Thanksgiving. It was just a normal Thursday to us. Besides, I used the time to finish my op-ed for December. It's about how the internet makes the world smaller. I wrote about how I get to talk online with my friends and family in India all the time, even though we live thousands of miles away from other."

"Neat," I said, thinking about how Maya's ajoba barely saw his family after he moved to America, since there was no internet then. Luckily, before I could feel myself getting sad again, the three of us began to walk down the street.

Oakridge's downtown was just around the corner from our neighborhood. Aai and Dad used to walk long distances to school as kids in India, so they never had any issues with me walking two streets down to the stores on Main Street in daylight when I was with Noah.

"Have you started brainstorming for your op-ed yet?" Avantika asked.

Noah shook his head on my behalf. "She thinks she doesn't have a strong opinion on anything."

"We're not all as lucky as you, Noah." I grinned. "You have a strong opinion about everything."

"You do too. I told you that before. You just choose not to share it," Noah said, picking up the pace. "Now come on, or it will close before we get there."

I sped up, thinking it was a good thing my bod-*Aai*-guard

wasn't here to slow us down. We were on a mission. Noah had written the first draft of his January op-ed for Mr. Crowe. Noah liked it so much, he wanted to mail it in to *Musings*, his favorite magazine, which published stuff written by kids. And we had to get it to the post office before they closed at 5:00 p.m. if he was going to meet their deadline for next month's edition.

I pulled the light-gray, bunny-eared hat Noah's dad had crocheted for me over my own ears and tried to get everyone to pick up the pace so my legs, which I was positive were now two icicles, would not break off. Avantika looked even worse than me. Her teeth were clattering against each other so loudly, she could barely even contribute to our conversation.

"Just think," said Noah, a frosty puff emerging from his mouth like he was a dragon. "In six weeks, I could be a published reporter."

"You are . . . published," Avantika said, shivering. "I . . . saw . . . your article . . . when I moved here. . . . Poop paintings . . . and swimming. . . . Remember?"

"You are so cold. Do you like bunnies? Or foxes? Those are pretty much the only two hats my dad can make," said Noah, pointing to his fox hat. "Or a sharkphin, but I highly suggest you not get a sharkphin."

I grinned at Noah and turned to Avantika. I didn't want "sharkphin" to turn into a "Breadstick Boy" inside joke. "It's that weird hat Noah wore when we first met you on Halloween."

"Ah," said Avantika, shivering even harder. "I'll . . . stick to . . . bunnies and foxes, then."

"Yeah, they're not perfect, but they're warm," said Noah. "You need a thicker hat if you're going to make it through this winter."

"Luckily, she doesn't have to suffer for too long," I said, sparing my molar-clanging friend some words.

"Oh, right," said Noah. "I almost forgot. India. Lucky you."

Avantika was lucky. So were Tanvi and Maya. They got to join the rest of the Desis in the country on their annual Christmas-break trip to India. Summer vacation was way longer, but India was just too hot then for a lot of the kids born here (and for Maya's ajoba). And the monsoon was during summer too. There were too many mosquitoes and stomach bugs during the monsoon.

We used to go every other year, on the odds, to India in December. It was such a strange feeling to leave Michigan freezing and get off the plane breathing in hot air in Mumbai, and I missed it. But a lot of doctors had left the clinic a few years ago, and Dad was working way more shifts than he normally did, including working almost every Christmas. So we had to skip the trip last December, when I was ten.

"Come on. Ten minutes to five," said Noah, glancing at his cell phone.

We jogged onto Main, rushing for the post office. There was a big line in front of it, ten people long, gathered by the streetlamp draped in a Christmas garland and bright red bow.

"You've got to be kidding," exclaimed Noah, throwing his hands into the air so quickly, he almost lost the manila envelope between the puffy, oversize fingers of his ski gloves. "Did the whole world decide to mail something on the exact day I need this to go out?"

But as we got closer, we quickly realized the people weren't in line for the post office. They were protesting in front of it. One wore a faded shirt with the union logo from the plant. The others had homemade signs and lawn signs for Abigail Winters. One man was as red as Aai's cranberry lonche as he led the chant: "Let me hear you shout! Foreigners, out!"

Avantika grabbed my elbow.

"This is what happens when hate goes unchecked," Noah muttered under his breath. "When people don't speak up."

"It's okay," I said, trying to convince myself as much as Avantika.

"Just run past them and don't look at them," said Noah, linking my other arm, as Avantika yanked the post office door open and we ran inside.

Even though the doors were closed and the heat was blowing loudly, we could still hear the chants outside the post office. Luckily, no one was in line except for one lady with a familiar-looking gray bun, who was looking over some pamphlets the protestors were handing out.

"Mrs. Finch?" asked Noah.

The lunch lady looked up from her reading. "Oh!" she said, recognizing us. She quickly hid the pamphlets in her purple wool coat's pocket. "Having a good evening?"

We nodded. Mrs. Finch went up to the counter for her turn, and Avantika and Noah began whispering about how scary the protestors outside were. But I couldn't participate. I was too busy staring at Mrs. Finch's pocket and wondering who else in our town had papers full of hate hidden in theirs.

SEVENTEEN

*T*hree weeks later a few snowflakes were finally falling, despite the unusually warm winter evening, during our last swim practice before my first swim meet as a Dolphin. It was also the start of Christmas break, and since Avantika was going to India for three weeks the afternoon of the meet, we had decided to have another sleepover tonight, this time at my house, right after practice, while her parents finished packing.

I put off thinking about what old movie I should ask Dad to find in his DVD collection for Avantika and me to watch and focused on the pool. The aqua-blue water was full of movement from all the relay teams and individual practices going on. But despite all that friction in the water, our two-hundred-yard-medley relay team was getting along great.

That's because we were swimming great. Harper and I were consistently within a second of our tryout times, if not matching them. Kendall's breaststroke form was getting better each week, and Aidy had gotten really fast at the fly, even better than she already was, if that was possible. She even beat Lizzie's old time on it. Coach Turner had no doubt we were going to beat our biggest competition, the Preston Porpoises, tomorrow at our first meet.

"We should celebrate," Aidy said as we fought off the post-shower shivers while changing into our sweats in the locker room.

They were navy blue with a gray dolphin over our hearts, and so plush that I felt like I was in a cocoon the moment I got the sweatshirt over my misshapen swim cap.

"How about a group dinner?" asked Kendall. "We could go to Joe's again."

Please. Not another Breadstick Boy joke I won't get to be a part of.

"I'm tired of Breadstick Boy," said Harper.

I breathed a little easier. Maybe they would pick someplace closer to home, and Aai could wait in the parking lot while I ate with my team before my sleepover with Avantika.

"How about the steak house?"

I closed my eyes and braced for the sharp stings all around my scalp as I pulled the swimming cap off as slowly as I could. The steak house was in downtown Oakridge, right around the corner from our house. But the steak house meant I'd be the one asking all the questions, and the answers would still make me look like an outsider as I interrogated the server to find out what broth was in the soup of the day, if the goat cheese had animal rennet in it, and if the fries had beef tallow, before eventually giving up and nibbling on some leaves while everyone else got to stuff themselves. I didn't want leaves. I was starving after this swim. Besides, I needed to get home for our sleepover, and Aai needed time to cook the popcorn on the stove like we lived in the 1980s or something.

"I have an even better idea," said Harper. "School's out. So why don't we order pizza and have a sleepover at my house? We're already in matching PJs," she added, modeling her Dolphins sweats.

"I'm not sure," I said, unzipping my duffel bag with the

bright purple advertisement for some medicine on it, which a pharmacy rep had given Dad.

"Is it your mom again? She is so strict," said Kendall, looking sympathetic.

"No, that's not it," I said. "I have something tonight."

"More important than team bonding?" asked Aidy, looking annoyed. "You can't keep missing team bonding. Is it some Indian thing again?"

I slouched in my spot, the burden of Aidy's words on my shoulders. "It's not that. I . . . I have another sleepover."

I felt my throat grow dry as I watched Aidy give Harper a look.

"With Noah?" Harper asked.

I shook my head. "Someone else."

"Who else could it possibly be?" Aidy asked, pulling her coat on.

I stared at the tiny tiles below my feet, envious of how similar they all were to each other. "Avantika."

Aidy's mouth dropped open. "Wow. It really is an Indian thing."

There they were. Those words that felt like an anchor, pulling me down. Like School Lekha, or any version of me, wasn't worthy of being included with Aidy. Like I wasn't good enough to be a part of her team because I was just too different. Just too Indian. My insides tightened into a knot as I stood there in silence.

"Come on, Aidy," Harper said, stuffing her towel into her wet-bag.

"What? At some point she has to decide." Aidy looked at me. "Do you want to fit in with us or do you want to fit in with her?"

Harper moved next to me. "It's before our first meet together. Teammates stick together, remember?"

I turned my back to the girls, grabbing my bobby pins from my bag. How was this happening? After a lifelong sleepover drought, it was finally a sleepover monsoon? Maya had gone to India once in the summer, right before school started, during the monsoon, and come home with a stomach bug. I could sympathize. My belly was aching during this downpour.

I had invited Avantika to my house. She was leaving for India the next day. We were going to pig out and watch movies and crack up just like we did at her house. But this was the first time anyone else from school had ever invited me for a sleepover. I wanted to fit in. And this was my team.

Teammates stuck together. And Aai had promised she would think about the next invite I got, if it was reasonable. Plus, Avantika was leaving for India the next day. She probably should be resting before her twenty-hour trip to India.

"Okay." I nodded, turning back to them, my bindi covered, as I forced a smile. "I'm in."

I rubbed my hand over my tummy, wondering just what I was going to say to get out of the sleepover with Avantika and convince my mom to let me go to the team sleepover, when my team practically crushed me in a group hug.

"Call her and cancel," Aidy said, drawing back from our huddle.

"I don't have a phone." I was stalling, but it was because I was starting to feel a little barfy, thinking about how to spare Avantika's feelings while still making sure Aidy, Kendall, and Harper really thought I was one of them.

"Lucky for you, I do." Kendall pulled her cell phone out of her pocket.

"Shouldn't I make sure my mom says yes first?"

"No." Aidy giggled. "What you should do first is cancel. Your mom already said yes to a sleepover tonight. What does it matter if the location and people at the sleepover change?"

I bet it would matter to Avantika if she found out, I thought as I pulled my emergency contact list out of my bag and found Avantika's number on it.

"Put it on speaker," Aidy added.

I nodded, my stomach feeling heavy. It was what Aai always told me to do when I used her cell phone, to avoid nuking my brain. But this felt different. This wasn't out of concern for my health. This was to hear someone else get hurt.

I tried to straighten my slouching spine a bit. "Sometimes there's too much static on speakerphone . . . ," I tried.

"Not Kenny's. It's brand-new," Aidy replied.

"Right." I looked over the keys on the shiny new phone, but my hand didn't budge. It was like it was so heavy, I couldn't move it. But I had to do this. Nothing I could say would change anyone's mind anyway. So I dialed, my belly throbbing when Avantika picked up.

"Hey, I'm pretty exhausted after practice."

Aidy giggled loudly until Harper elbowed her. "Shh!"

"What was that?" asked Avantika on the other end.

"Nothing. I'm at the pool. Anyway, I'm really tired and . . . and we have our big meet tomorrow. Would you mind if we canceled tonight?"

Avantika paused. I felt terrible. She was disappointed. But after a breath I could hear her smiling on the phone again.

"Totally. I understand. I should probably help my parents pack anyway."

I exhaled. The lie had worked. And Avantika would never know everyone heard me cancel on her.

"I'll see you before you leave tomorrow," I added, trying to remind myself I was a good friend.

"Sounds great. Bye!"

"Bye!" shouted Aidy, before doubling over the bench in a fit of giggles.

"Who said that—"

I hung up as fast as I could.

"Easy-peasy," said Harper, heading around the lockers to the exit. "Now just tell your mom plans have changed."

Still feeling a little nauseated, I rushed out to Aai, who was waiting by the lobby desk by herself, since Dad was still at the clinic. I looked back. Aidy, Kendall, and their parents started talking to Harper's mom by the exit. It was like Diwali all over again.

"Avantika isn't coming over tonight," I said shakily, even though that part wasn't a lie.

"She's not?"

I shook my head, trying to sound as natural as I could. "I forgot to tell you. They're busy packing," I added, a little shocked at how easy it was to come up with such a big fib. "And lucky for me, my team is having a sleepover at Harper's tonight. And you promised you'd think about letting me go."

"If the circumstances were right," Aai said. "You know I don't like you sleeping at a stranger's."

"She's not a stranger. I've gone to school with her forever. She lives by the river. And it's not Diwali. Or Sankrant, or Holi, or Gudhi Padwa, or Ganpati, or any of the other hundreds of holidays we have. Please?"

"Give me a minute to think, Lekha."

"If I keep missing team events, how can I be part of the team? Please. I just want to be normal, like everyone else."

Aai sighed as we neared Harper and her mom under the exit sign. "You are normal. But you're not like everyone else. You're you."

"You coming?" asked Harper, hopping impatiently from foot to foot.

I looked at Aai, who began the eternity-long process of introducing herself, explaining we were vegetarian, and asking if Harper's mom kept any guns in the house. Mrs. Walbourne looked annoyed when Aai followed up with, "Are you sure?" But after the Walbournes passed the test, Aai patted me on the head and said, "I hope you girls have a great time tonight."

I beamed. "I'll pack my stuff and see you guys soon," I said, waving to Harper as I ran across the frosty parking lot and got into our car.

"It's just too bad Avantika couldn't join you guys," said Aai as she started the car.

I looked outside the foggy window, running my finger across the cold glass to draw my cow on it. Just like the condensation I wiped off the window, my excitement disappeared too, as the guilty feeling started churning at my intestines again. Where was that delicious digestive when I needed it?

Oh, right. At Avantika's house.

EIGHTEEN

*A*s the lights twinkled brightly on the large artificial Christmas tree in the family room behind us, I stared at the table full of food laid out before me, Kendall, Aidy, Harper, and Harper's six-year-old brother, Harrison, in the Walbournes' small kitchen. It was loaded with candy and chocolate and an extra-large cheese pizza. I smiled, thinking about how Dad used to teach me the order of the planets by reciting a song that said, "My very educated mother just served us nine pizza pies." After I reminded Dad that Pluto had gotten kicked out of the planet club, he ordered a "pizza pie" in its honor, and since then, every time Aai made pizza, Dad would start the meal by holding his slice up against ours as if we were clinking glasses, but instead of "Cheers," he'd say, "To our dear friend in the sky, good old pizza pie."

I reached for a can of pop in between bites of piping hot pizza. Aai normally had us avoid cans because of some chemical they leached, but she wasn't here and I was thirsty.

Seated by the sliding-glass door, through which I could just barely make out the river in the darkness, Harper was wrapping a gooey strand of cheese around her finger like a bandage. "We have to beat Preston tomorrow. They beat us at every swim meet last year. Tomorrow, it stops."

"For sure," said Kendall, chewing on some candy. "Hey!"

Harrison swiped the candy off Kendall's plate and put it on his pizza. Kendall playfully rubbed Harrison's blond hair as he swallowed his mutant pizza down.

"That is disgusting," laughed Aidy.

"He's always putting the grossest stuff on his pizza," said Harper.

"You ladies want anything else to eat?" asked Mrs. Walbourne from the kitchen.

"No, thanks," I said as the fizz from the pop tickled my throat.

"Mm-kay," she responded, her head inside the fridge.

I gasped when I saw the large navy-blue magnet on the open refrigerator door. It said, DON'T LIKE IT?

"What's wrong?" asked Harper.

"Bit my tongue," I lied. My third lie of the night. I was getting to be a little too good at this. But if Mrs. Walbourne had a Winters magnet up, did that mean she didn't like me? That she thought my parents were stealing everyone's jobs? I tried to figure out a way to casually mention the fact that Aai no longer worked at the plant, but Harrison spoke up first.

"What are you getting for Christmas?" he asked.

"I don't know, Harrison. Santa hasn't come to my house yet," said Aidy.

"I'm getting LEGOs," Harrison responded, in between bites of chocolate cheese.

"What do you want Santa to bring you, Lekha?" asked Aidy. "Sorry. Is it against your religion to celebrate Christmas?"

I took a big gulp of pop, hoping I wouldn't burp from all the bubbles I was swallowing. "It's not against my religion. But it's not really a holiday for my religion," I said softly, hoping Mrs. Walbourne wasn't going to say something to me.

"Yeah, Hindi people celebrate Diwali," said Harper, trying to show off what she had heard in Mr. Crowe's class, not realizing she had said the language, Hindi, instead of the religion, Hindu.

But as usual, I didn't speak up to correct her. I just nodded, reaching for another slice of pizza, wishing the topic of conversation would change. We did have a Christmas tree, but only because I begged Dad to get me one after I'd helped decorate Noah's year after year. Aai spent way too much time worrying about the flame retardants in the prelit plastic trees and eventually compromised on getting a potted rosemary plant shaped like a Christmas tree from a store. We would decorate it each December and let it hang out in the Jungle for the rest of the year. But I didn't get a ton of Christmas presents. I got one from my parents, and then Noah and I exchanged one too.

After dinner the four of us took our turns in the bathroom, brushing our teeth and getting ready for bed. Then we went into Harper's room. Harper's room was a lot like my room. No computer, off-white walls, a lot of books, and posters and calendars everywhere, except instead of posters of Aamir Khan and Hindu gods, she had posters of bands and Wonder Woman.

I had a brief moment of panic when Kendall began to braid Aidy's hair, hoping no one had Googled sleepovers like Avantika had and wanted to braid my hair, but no one asked, and I didn't mention it. All I knew was I would be dealing with a bunch of knots in my hair the next morning that would need a ton of oil and Aai brushing to untangle them. Because I wasn't getting a chance to put it into a bunch of braids myself. But I didn't want to deal with them seeing my birthmark, or putting a comb in my hair and seeing it get stuck. And I definitely didn't want someone to ask what stank when I put coconut oil in my braids.

As the lights went off in Harper's mom's room, where she and Harrison were sleeping, our voices dropped to a whisper.

"You guys, I know how we can make sure we beat Preston tomorrow," said Aidy, reaching into her backpack. We all leaned in to see what the secret weapon was going to be. Aidy pulled out a pink plastic razor.

Kendall began to giggle. "What are you talking about?"

"Didn't you watch the Olympics? Professional swimmers

shave their legs and arms. It cuts seconds off their times."

"I doubt it helps that much," said Harper, glancing at her mother's door.

"Sure, it does," said Aidy, typing frantically on Kendall's phone. "See? It makes you more aerodynamic."

We all scanned the article she had brought up about shaving and swimming.

"Besides, I already shave my legs when I wear shorts. My mom let me start in fifth grade," said Aidy.

"I'm not shaving my arms," said Kendall. "My dad's face is super rough from shaving. I don't want my arms to feel that way."

"You barely even have hair on your arms," said Aidy.

I played with the elastic cuffs on the ends of the Dolphins sweatshirt, grateful my arms weren't showing.

"So, what do you say?" asked Aidy. "Teammates stick together, right? We want to win tomorrow, right? Your first time representing the Dolphins at a meet?" she asked, looking at me and Harper.

Harper quickly nodded.

I wanted to shake my head. I wanted to say no. But my lips wouldn't move. Instead, I grabbed the razor. It was lighter than I had expected, and yet everything about it felt like it was weighing me down and I was sinking.

I watched as the two strips of metal glistened in the light from Harper's lamp. The blades looked sharp. I wondered if it would hurt. I wondered if I would have little specks of toilet paper pressed against the dabs of blood on my legs the way Dad sometimes had to do to his chin, cheeks, and neck.

But if all it took was a little bit of pain to finally be accepted, to finally be just like everyone else, whether it was on the team or at school, maybe it was worth keeping my mouth shut and just doing it?

Aidy grinned, and my head started to feel like a brick. I suddenly wished I hadn't lied my way out of a sleepover with Avantika. I had already lied to my mom, Avantika, and my teammates today. I didn't want to do anything else wrong. And I knew Aai would have been really mad if I shaved before she said I could. She always said kids grow up way too fast in America. She got mad once at the dentist's when she saw me reading a teen magazine about crushes. If tomorrow she saw I had shaved, she'd be furious. So I put the razor down and, despite it being almost as light as a feather, I felt a weight being lifted away as I shook my head. Like it actually felt good to stand up for myself for once, even though I knew what was coming next.

"You of all people aren't doing it?" snapped Aidy, any trace of her smile gone.

"Aidy!" said Kendall, grabbing the razor. "Don't worry about it, Lekha."

"No, she should worry about it," said Aidy.

"Shh!" begged Harper, glancing around the room as if the door weren't closed and her mom was standing right in front of us, hearing about the top-secret shaving plans.

"My parents don't want me to shave yet," I said, certain I sounded younger than Harrison.

"Aren't you sick of people telling you you need a lawn mower? Or calling you Broom? This is how to stop it," Aidy said, pointing to the razor. "Plus, you'll guarantee we win."

The only way to stop being called Broom was to shave? I wanted to yell back at Aidy that she was the only one who called me Broom, so if she just stopped saying it, it would stop. I wanted to remind her I'd already done something against my mom's rules when I had lied to come to this sleepover. I wanted to tell her we had already swum our fastest times and we all had hair on our bodies when we did it.

I wanted desperately to say all of this. Maybe I'd feel even less burdened than I had felt a moment ago. But instead, I just stood there as Aidy sighed dramatically at me, like I was some annoying outsider ruining everything for her.

"I'm really tired," I said, changing the subject. "You guys can do it. I'm going to bed." I scooched down into my sleeping bag, putting the cover over my face so they wouldn't see the tear that had slipped out. I knew that dealing with how upset Aai would be if I shaved would be only slightly worse than dealing with how upset my teammates were right now. I tried not to let any more tears break free as Kendall, Harper, and Aidy shaved their legs in the closed bathroom. Every few seconds, in between the whispers and grumbles I was positive were about me, I heard someone say, "Ouch," and Harper shush them before adding her own, "Ow!"

I was so mad at myself for blowing off Avantika. I knew she would never have made me feel bad for not doing something I didn't feel comfortable doing. I'd be watching Hindi movies with her and laughing if I hadn't canceled on her. I had made a mistake. No. It was worse than that. I had conned my way out of hanging out with a good friend. And

I let everyone watch as I canceled on her. I deserved to be miserable right now.

I rolled onto my side and held the top of my sleeping bag tightly over my ears, trying to drown out the yelps of team bonding in the bathroom. I wiped my nose, sniffling, my chest heavy. I didn't have to say "ouch" or "ow" like my teammates to know how badly I was hurting.

chapter

NINETEEN

The next morning I got ready and ate breakfast with the rest of the team, my hair full of knots. It was a much quieter meal than our dinner had been. Aidy, Kendall, and Harper didn't say anything about shaving to me, probably because Harper didn't want her mom to find out what they had done. Or maybe because they were trying to hide the hobbling caused by all their cuts. Dad and the rest of the parents came to get us soon after breakfast so we could have time to recoup before the meet, and I practically bolted to the car after saying bye.

"Did you have fun with your new friends?" asked Dad as the car drove alongside the snakelike river that coiled its way around this part of Oakridge. "Or should I say, 'pod'?"

I watched the small houses on the drab riverbank, under the gloomy December sky, blur by us.

"Get it? A pod is a group of dolphins," Dad said, taking the turn off the dirt road onto pavement.

"Pod" is probably a more realistic term for us than "friends," I thought, eager to get home to see my real friends.

I pulled one of my sweatpants legs up, looking at the fine black hairs on my skin. I ran my hand up and down my bony leg. The hair felt fuzzy and soft. But it was definitely visible. I thought back to Liam laughing at me at tryouts as we pulled onto our street.

I quickly shoved my pant leg back down. Avantika and her parents were in their driveway, loading their bags into their car. Aai was heading down the porch steps, probably to say bye to them. My hand began to sweat as I gripped the car door handle, waiting for Dad to pull into the driveway so I could stop her from spilling the beans about my sleepover.

The rickety garage door started opening as Aai headed down our walkway to the driveway.

"I really should oil that," said Dad. "Remind me tomorrow."

"Okay," I said. "Can I get out?"

Aai was a couple of steps from our car.

"Missed Aai that much?" laughed Dad, unlocking the door. "She'll be glad to hear that."

"Something like that," I said, hopping out.

Aai hugged me. "How was it?"

"Great!" I said. I guessed I could add that to my lie tally. So much for being a good Desi kid.

"I'm going to say bye to the Savarkars. Want to come?" she asked as Dad neared us.

I nodded, digging my fingers under my jacket collar to put my Dolphins hood over my head. "Just don't tell her where I was last night. I don't want her to feel bad since she couldn't have a sleepover."

Forget Broom and Dot. I had a new name for myself. Liar. And it almost felt worse than the others.

I ran across the street to Avantika, who stood before six large suitcases and three carry-ons her parents were trying to fit into their little sedan.

"Where are you coming back from?" she asked, waving to me.

"I was at a . . . team thing," I said. That was actually the truth. For once. "Ready for India?" I asked as my parents started helping Avantika's in a game of suitcase Tetris.

"I'm so excited. I could use the break from this freezing weather!" She shivered.

I nodded. I didn't have the heart to tell her this was nothing, that normally we had lots of snow in December, or that January and February would be way worse.

"I wish you were here for our neighbor dinner with Noah's family tomorrow. You'd have fun. We do it every Christmas break when Noah's parents are off for shutdown."

Avantika looked confused.

"Plant shutdown. The car factories. When they're closed, anyone who works there is off too, so Noah's parents are on vacation then. And my mom used to be too, when she worked at the plant, so they started this tradition every year we don't go to India. We always go to What's the Mattar?, even if it's snowing, as long as the roads are okay."

Avantika giggled in between her teeth chattering. "What did you say?"

"What's the Mattar? They make the best mattar paneer. And they have hilarious Hindi jokes all over their menu. What did the happy pea say to the sad pea?"

Avantika grinned. "Oh. What's the *mattar*," she said, emphasizing the Hindi word for peas.

"What did the brother carrot say to the sister carrot?"

"Gaajar . . . I don't know."

"Gaajar annoying. Like, God, you're annoying. Get it?" I continued as Avantika laughed. "And here's Noah's favorite. What did the cheese say to the corn chip at the dance party?"

"Nacho!" Avantika exclaimed, saying the Hindi word for dance. "That is hilarious. There should be some Marathi jokes like that."

"There should be, but there aren't. We'll have to invent them."

"I'll work on some on the plane rides, and you can do it over break."

"Deal." I smiled, suddenly feeling a tightening in my throat. It was the feeling I got every time we said bye to my family in India. It was the worst, saying bye to your grandparents, aunts, uncles, and cousins after getting to spend a few days being close to them and getting close with them. Bending down to do namaskar to your elders, trying not to cry as you glance at the wrinkles on their feet, knowing it may be the last time you ever get to hug them, the last time you ever get to see them. Avantika was going for only three weeks, but I knew I was going to miss her, and I knew I hadn't been a good friend to her lately. I gave her an awkward hug, wishing that I could fly on the plane with my friend instead of having to swim with my pod.

chapter

TWENTY

That evening, with Avantika gone, I sat next to Harper, Kendall, and Aidy on the cold metal bleachers, watching the rest of the Dolphins swim their events. We were in our dark-blue Dolphins swimsuits, and I kept my towel over my lap, hoping no one would notice the hair on my legs. When my teammates were cheering on the divers, I snuck a quick glance at their legs. They were hair-free, except for some patches they had missed, but they were also covered with dozens of little red lines. Cuts.

"My knee kills," whispered Kendall.

"Don't be a baby. It's like a paper cut," said Aidy.

"Like five hundred paper cuts all over my knees and legs," muttered Kendall. "My sister laughed when she saw me this morning. She said you're supposed to use water and soap to shave. Not just drag a razor across dry legs."

Harper raised an eyebrow at Aidy. "You said you'd done this before."

Coach Turner waved for us to take our places. Aidy stood up, her cheeks red, and started loosening up in stretches as she led us to our lane.

I glanced over, sizing up our competition. The Electric Eels, Dragons, Sharks, and Rockets were stretching, goggles on, looking fierce, but I wasn't worried. They weren't as good as us. The only team I was worried about was several lanes away: the Preston Porpoises.

My belly felt like it was flickering on and off like that broken light in our cafeteria. I turned back to the stands. Aai had the camcorder out, ready to record my every move. Dad stood up and made his way down closer to me. "Lekha. Lekha!"

I could feel my ears getting hotter. "I can hear you, Dad."

Some people in the audience snickered.

"Himmat karke," he mouthed to me, sensing my embarrassment.

I took a deep breath in, trying to be brave. ". . . Badha kadam," I mouthed back to him.

Satisfied, Dad returned on his apology tour, stepping over people as he went back up to his spot next to Aai, and my team closed in for a huddle with our coach.

"Stay focused," Coach Turner said. "Breathe. You're a new team, but you are one of the best I've ever coached."

Aidy added her part of the pep talk. "We are going to beat them. We're faster. We know we are." She nodded at Harper and Kendall before turning to me with an ever-so-quick look of annoyance.

"Dolphins on three," said Coach as we followed his lead and roared our team name.

Harper got in the water, preparing for the backstroke, as Kendall, Aidy, and I took our positions. The buzzer sounded and Harper was off, kicking her legs, her arms moving smoothly with each commanding stroke. She turned at the far end, almost half a pool length ahead of everyone else, including Preston. We cheered as she hit the wall, and Kendall dove in, her head bobbing in the water with each breath and stride.

She had a huge lead thanks to Harper, but she wasn't moving her legs as fast as normal, and in between the foam, I could see her cringing, like she was in pain.

"Hurry up, Kenny! They're gaining on you!" shouted Aidy, hopping nervously in place.

Kendall began to kick faster, but the Rockets, Dragons, and Porpoises were nearing her. And soon the Preston swimmer overtook her.

"You can do it, Kendall!" I shouted.

It didn't seem to help. The Porpoises and Dragons were now ahead of her, and their swimmers dove in before Kendall reached Aidy.

Kendall finally touched the wall at the same time as the swimmer from the Rockets. Aidy and the Rockets' butterfly swimmer dove in at the same time. But Aidy was determined. She sped forward, ahead of the Rockets, almost catching up to the Porpoises and Dragons.

Their swimmers dove in for the freestyle, and a couple of seconds later Aidy tapped the wall and I went in.

Icy water hit me all around, but I focused and breathed my way forward until my body and the waves felt like one. I had to catch up. I could do this, I thought as I churned my arms forward. I was strong. My arms were strong. My legs were strong. I had no cuts to stop me. Aidy did, and she still swam faster than anyone in the pool. I could do this.

I tried to see where the other swimmers were in the split second it took to turn my head to take a breath. But I couldn't see them. I tried to fight through the burning muscles. Push forward. I reminded myself again, my arms were strong. My legs were strong. I had no cuts to stop me. . . . Just leg hair to slow me down.

My legs suddenly started to feel like lead. There was that weight again. The sinking feeling I couldn't shake off when it came to wanting desperately to impress Aidy.

"Keep going, Lekha!" Harper screamed.

I tapped the edge and turned. My arms moved like a windmill as I shoved ahead. Fatigue began to fill my muscles, but I kept going. Fighting the feeling that I was dragging an anchor under me, I hit the wall and pulled my goggles off, ready to hear a bunch of cheers.

I did. But they were coming from the other side of the bench. The Porpoises had won. The Dragons were second. The Rockets, third. I was a second shy of my best time. Kendall was several seconds off her average. I pulled myself out of the water and took the towel from Coach.

"Good swim, Lekha," said Harper, patting my shoulder.

"You did great," added Kendall.

Coach nodded. "You did well, guys. The other teams did a little better. We have a couple of months before conference finals. We'll get there. Dry off and shake hands."

I dried my arms and bent down to dry my legs.

"You're in America now," Aidy said softly, her eyes hardening.

I looked up. Now? Where was I before?

"Tell your mom eleven is not too young to shave in America."

Aidy turned to shake hands with the Dragons next to us.

I stood up to join the congratulatory line, smiling and shaking hands with the other swimmers. I wasn't in the water anymore, Aidy's heavy words weighing me down, but I couldn't shake the feeling I was drowning.

chapter

TWENTY-ONE

I spent the rest of the first weekend of Christmas break enjoying what it was a break from. No school, and no swimming. Nothing to stress about. Nothing to lie about. Nothing to worry about. I was back to being a good Desi girl.

I spent the day reading books and watching TV, and it was at last time for our neighbors' dinner. I waited impatiently, visions of mattar paneer dancing in my head, as Aai and Dad got ready. I chewed on a soft garlic clove that Aai had soaked in yogurt and then sautéed in toop. It was an ayurvedic tonic. A garlic clove a day keeps the doctor away. It almost tasted like garlic bread, and I loved it. I grabbed the container to get another clove when the house phone rang.

I reached for it. "Hello?"

"Merry Christmas!" said a cheery woman on the other end.

"Merry Christmas," I replied.

"My name is Karen, and I'm calling on behalf of Winters for Congress. May I know who I have the pleasure of speaking to?"

"Lekha Divekar," I responded, not sure if I should hang up or keep talking.

"Wow! What a beautiful name."

I sighed. "Thanks." I knew what was coming next.

"Where are you from?"

There it was. The question that filled me with the feeling of being less than. Of not belonging. Like the person asking it had every right to decide who was American and who wasn't. "Michigan," I replied as Aai and Dad came down the stairs ready to go.

The woman chuckled. "No, where are you really from?"

"India," I said, giving up. I knew this was the answer she wanted the second the awful question left her lips, because to her, there was no way a person with a name like mine could be from here. "And I have to go. Sorry. Bye," I blurted before hanging up.

But before I could put our phone back on the counter, Dad's cell phone rang.

He picked it up and I watched his eyebrows move together. "What happened?" He spotted me staring at him and quickly lowered his voice.

"Let's get our shoes on," said Aai.

"But what about Dad?"

"Sounds like some work stuff. We'll wait for him in the car."

◎ ◎

Dad was barely talking as we drove down to Detroit. He got that way sometimes when he was worrying about a patient, so Aai and I tried to pick out what we would order in addition to mattar paneer. But the menu was not loading on What's the Mattar?'s website.

When we entered the restaurant, which was filled with the scent of creamy tomato sauce, Dad told the hostess we were meeting some friends. We spotted Noah's family sitting in a booth near a giant painting of the old movie star Amitabh Bachchan and headed that way.

We passed several Indian families enjoying their meal and one large table with a white family. I wondered if the hostess had led the Wades to them when they first arrived at the restaurant, the way it always happened to us at an American restaurant. If Aai was inside getting our table while Dad and I found parking, and then we got there, before we could even open our mouths, the host or hostess would always ask, "Are you meeting a woman here?" And they'd lead us to Aai. They just assumed the brown people were together, and I guess in our case, they were right. But it was still annoying.

At the restaurant Noah and I exchanged our Christmas gifts. Noah had gotten me a set of watercolor pencils to amp up my cow-drawing game. I watched as Noah opened his present.

"What a gorgeous frame, Lekha," said Mrs. Wade, sipping on her mango lassi.

"It's to frame your *Musings* article next month," I said.

Noah's cheeks turned pink. "That's so cool. Thanks. I haven't heard back from them yet, but I'm hoping it's there."

"It will be," I said as the waitress returned with copper vessels full of mattar paneer and samosas with green chutney and my favorite chincha chutney. She made a second trip to get the bhaat, daal, other vegetables, and a bread basket with plain naan, garlic naan, onion kulcha, and aloo paratha, bursting at the seams with its potato stuffing.

Dad's cell phone rang loudly just as I was dipping my samosa into the dark-brown chutney and watching the chin-cha get soaked up into the fried dough. He excused himself and stepped away, by the front doors, to take the call.

"Work issues," Aai said, smiling apologetically at the Wades. "I ran into Mary Beth at the grocery store the other day," she said as they began their usual reminiscing from when Aai still worked with Mr. and Mrs. Wade at the plant. "She said she retired! I thought she'd never retire."

Noah's dad laughed. "She was one tough union president! Always ready to fight for autoworkers' rights."

Aai nodded. "She said the union is split fifty-fifty. People are out of work and looking for someone to blame. I worry for us if Winters wins."

Noah's mom shook her head. "She's not going to win, hon. Hate cannot win."

I thought about the signs sweeping across my neigh-borhood. About the pamphlet in Mrs. Finch's pocket. About the magnet on my teammate's fridge door. And suddenly I started to sweat. I wiped my hands on my napkin and exchanged a glance with Noah.

His face was shiny, his eyes were large and serious, and his lips were twisted to the side. "But what if she does win?"

"We'll deal with that if the day comes, bud," said Noah's dad. He was sweating too, and I couldn't tell if it was from the food or from the talk about Winters. Mr. Wade wiped his forehead with his napkin and looked at me and my mom, his eyes as wide as Noah's, as his own lips also twisted to the side. "We all will."

chapter
TWENTY-TWO

*A*ai drove us back to Oakridge. Dad was checking his cell phone every few minutes on the ride, calling other doctor friends to ask them questions about orbital lobes and concussion and words I couldn't pronounce, let alone remember. Back in the house, he had been taking calls in the Jungle on and off for the past hour, ever since we got back.

I watched an old black-and-white Christmas movie on the family room TV while eating some spicy and sweet ginger vadi, a treat I got during winter. I was humming along softly to the Christmas music when Dad entered the kitchen.

I had never seen him take this many phone calls for work from home. And his face looked different from normal, like his cheeks were drained of color. I watched as he plugged his phone in near a panoramic picture from India. On its left was a Zoroastrian fire temple in a neighborhood lined by crowded shops, and a synagogue by a cluster of trees. In the middle were rows of bungalows, a mosque, schools, a temple, and towering apartment buildings with the silhouette of a kid flying a kite on one of the terraces. On a hill in the background was a Buddha statue, and just a little bit away, under a flock of birds, was a church. Every bit of the city was drenched in the pink and peach glow of the sunset. Dad almost knocked the peaceful picture over as he set his phone down distractedly and opened the microwave to nuke his tea.

It was a habit of his that always annoyed Aai. He would make the most amazing tea with homegrown lemongrass and ginger, but he said the milk cooled the boiled tea down too much. So he would insist on microwaving it, even though it was already hot.

Aai moved away from the range of the microwave and touched Dad's phone. "It's so hot. Is everything okay at work?"

Lost in thought, Dad took his tea out of the microwave and sipped at it.

"Hello?" Aai asked, annoyed.

Dad glanced at me and went into the living room. Aai followed. I could barely catch a word Dad was saying, so I tiptoed into the kitchen to hear better. But then Aai started crying.

"What? When? Why didn't you tell me?"

My stomach sank. I knew what this was. Dad had gotten a call from India. A relative had died, thousands of miles away. I started to cry, thinking of Aaji, as I ran to the living room.

"Who died? You can't keep it a secret forever!" I said, my nose running.

My parents turned to me, shocked.

"Don't cry, beta," said Dad, wiping my tears with his sleeve. "Nobody died."

"Then why is Aai crying? What happened?"

Aai sniffled as she looked at Dad.

"I'm not a baby anymore. Just tell me!"

"It's Ajay Mama."

"What about him?" I asked, thinking of my uncle in California.

Dad squeezed my shoulder. "This evening Veena Mami called to tell me Mama is in the hospital. I didn't tell you because I didn't want to upset Aai until I knew more. He and his friend Joginder Uncle, remember him? With the two girls you used to play with when we would go to Berkeley?"

I nodded. They sent me their hand-me-down Indian clothes with Ajay Mama the last time he visited. I wore their salwar-kurta to Diwali.

"Well, Uncle and Ajay Mama went out to a movie, and as they were nearing the theater, some men forced them off the road and beat them. Badly."

"Did they rob them?"

Dad shook his head. "The police are calling it a hate crime. The men broke one of Ajay Mama's ribs and his eye was hurt badly, but Veena Mami just called to say the doctors were able to save it. Joginder Uncle's turban was pulled off and he has a concussion, but he will be okay too."

I couldn't believe it. Joginder Uncle wore a turban to signify equality and to remember the teachings of his Sikh faith. How could someone forcibly remove it? And how could someone hurt Uncle and Ajay Mama like this?

"Ajay Mama just got out of surgery and he's resting. But we will call him tomorrow to check on him, okay?"

"What will my mother think?" asked Aai over the sound

of the TV. "She's going to be so worried. We have to find her a flight."

"Veena asked us not to say anything to her," said Dad, heading to the family room to turn down the volume on the TV, Aai and me behind him. "We don't want to make her sick."

We weren't going to tell my grandmother what had happened to her own son? We were all just going to keep quiet when Aaji called from India, and change the subject to things like the weather and what we were eating?

I frowned as I watched Aai sob into her hands, defeated, remembering what Mrs. Wade had said at dinner just a few hours earlier. She was wrong. We all were wrong.

Hate had won.

chapter

TWENTY-THREE

*M*y night-light always made the pleats in my purple curtains cast a strange shadow on my wall. When I was younger, it used to creep me out, because the shadow looked like a monster with horns and sharp teeth. Somewhere around fourth grade, I realized it was all in my head. There were no monsters in real life. But tonight, as I tried to sleep, all I could think about was the monster who attacked my poor mama and Joginder Uncle. Could that monster come to my town too and hurt my parents or me? I tossed and turned all night over that question, feeling hot, feeling cold, but most of all, feeling scared.

In the morning Aai served me a bowl of hot oatmeal with raisins. The raisins were plump from the milk. But something else was swollen too. Aai had bags under her eyes, like she had slept even less than me. Like she had been crying a lot.

Dad, who had been up late talking to Mami and the surgeons in California, walked up to us with a phone and a smile on his face. "It's Ajay."

"Put it on FaceTime," I said. I needed to see that my uncle was okay.

I saw Aai and Dad exchange a glance. "Not right now. He's recovering from eye surgery," Aai whispered, before putting the cell on speakerphone.

I spoke to my uncle, who promised us he was not in a lot of pain. Dad used to complain about how loud Ajay Mama was. He had this booming, friendly voice, and would strike up a conversation with strangers everywhere we went. When we went to the Redwood National Park, his voice echoed, bouncing off the trees as he asked every hiker we passed how their day was going and what was the coolest thing they had seen. His voice filled the restaurants we would go to as he would lean over to make jokes with strangers at the tables next to us. But today his voice sounded different as he told us he and Joginder Uncle were okay. And I don't think it was because it was so early in California compared to Michigan. He was quieter, his voice shaking, the way I knew I sounded after a puking bug had made me exhausted. It was weird hearing someone so vivacious suddenly have his voice weakened.

I sniffled loudly. As Aai said she wanted us to fly out to California to help with Ajay Mama's rehab, and Veena Mami insisted they would manage, my throat hurt a little, like I was about to cry. It was as if that monster from my wall had come to life, and no amount of daylight would make it disappear.

Dad patted my head softly. "Why don't you go over to Noah's? They're expecting you. We're just going to make sure Ajay Mama is all set to leave the hospital in a few days."

I nodded, feeling grateful for the chance to temporarily escape the monster, and headed next door.

I was greeted with a huge hug from Mrs. Wade, who was sniffling even louder than I had been. "Oh, Lekha. I'm so sorry. How are they?"

"They're okay." I shrugged, bending down to pet Cookie.

Noah walked out of the kitchen with two steaming mugs. He sat on the stairs and I plopped down next to him, grateful for the hot cocoa.

"No marshmallows in yours," Noah said softly. "It's gelatin-free."

I gave him a small smile, wishing there were more people like Noah in this world and fewer people like whoever attacked Ajay Mama and Joginder Uncle.

"How's your grandma, hon?" Mrs. Wade asked, leaning on the banister.

I shrugged again. "They're not telling her."

"They're not?" Noah looked appalled. He was always a stickler for the truth. I was lucky he didn't know what I had done to Avantika with the sleepover a few days ago.

"She's old, Noah," said Mrs. Wade. "And she's far away in another country. Sometimes . . . sometimes we withhold information for the sake of someone's health."

"Oh." Noah stared into his mug. "I guess that makes sense. I wouldn't want her to have a heart attack or get sick from worrying about your uncle."

I nodded, drinking the piping-hot cocoa despite how it burned my throat. "I think sometimes there's a good reason for not saying stuff."

Noah's brow furrowed, like he was struggling to make sense of it all. "I was wrong."

I looked at Noah. I wasn't sure what he was about to say, but I wasn't in the mood to dissect what had happened to Joginder Uncle and Ajay Mama like an unbiased journalist observing it all from a distance. This wasn't like a story Noah wrote for the paper. This was my story. And I didn't want to keep reliving it.

"You're right. It's not always safe to speak up. Maybe sometimes you need someone else to speak up who wouldn't be in danger because of it."

I watched the steam rise from my mug and fade away like a whisper. "I don't want to talk about the op-ed. And I don't want to talk about my uncle anymore." I stopped, looking at Mrs. Wade. "If that's okay."

"Of course, hon," she said, rubbing my shoulder.

I sat next to Noah, a hand on Cookie's head, and just stared at the frosty world outside the front door without saying a word. It wasn't a comfortable silence. It wasn't a heavy silence. It wasn't a silence that spoke volumes. It was just silence. And it was what I needed.

chapter
TWENTY-FOUR

*A*s the days went by over break, Ajay Mama and Joginder Uncle got better and better. We called Aaji and talked to her about snow and what we were going to cook for dinner, avoiding the topic of my uncle altogether. We even managed to cheer Aai up enough to put our little rosemary Christmas tree up, and on Christmas morning I woke up to a new Aamir Khan poster and the news that Joginder Uncle and Ajay Mama had been released from the hospital. I loved Aamir Khan, but clearly the news that everyone was okay was the best present of the day.

Each day seemed to bring with it a new bit of good news. Ajay Mama's bandages came off and his vision was improving. Joginder Uncle's bruising was almost totally gone, and he was able to go back to work. Mama finally discovered podcasts while his eye healed. But he was back to talking so much, Veena Mami could barely understand what was going on in the podcasts. . . .

And my nights were finally better too. I moved my night-light to another wall, and the shadowy monster was gone for good, so on New Year's Eve, I woke up refreshed and ready to stay up late to ring in the new year.

I helped Aai mix the dough for the pizzas we always ate at New Year's, pouring in the spelt, whole wheat, and all-purpose flours, and the flaxseed meal. Dad was cutting up red bell peppers and onions, and boiling corn.

"Aren't you sick of corn pizza?" he asked as he leaned over the stove to check on the kernels skidding around in the bubbling water.

"Never," I replied. It was like my peanut butter and jelly sandwiches at school. When I found something I liked, I stuck with it.

"It reminds her of India," Aai added, putting a glass lid over the mixing bowl so our dough would rise.

"Remember that restaurant in Pune where we first had it?"

Aai nodded. "I'm pretty sure that's the same restaurant

where we first had a cheese dosa when you were little."

I washed the remnants of the flour and oil off my hands, remembering the first time I bit into a piping-hot crepe filled with melted Indian cheese instead of the potatoes and onions masala dosas normally had.

"Clearly a very innovative place," Aai said with a tiny smile.

"You all left that restaurant with full bellies. I left with a headache because Ajay decided to lead the restaurant in a game of Antakshari. The noise that day! And I'm not talking about the singing. I'm talking about that loud voice of your brother's," Dad laughed.

Aai did too, before quickly looking away.

Dad cleared his throat. "You have an hour before that dough rises, Lekha. Why don't you work on your homework? Aai told me you have an article due in a few weeks. Might as well get a head start, right?"

I shrugged. If only Dad knew how many weeks ago I had been assigned this homework, he may not have thought about today as a head start. But I headed upstairs anyway. After all the bad things that had happened around here, I was on a mission to make things easier on Aai. To make sure my days on the wrong side of the unspoken Desi-kid law were far behind me.

So up I went. I tapped my pencil on my desk and looked at the pleats of my purple curtains, counting them, guessing their width, and every once in a while trying to figure out what I was going to write.

The last idea I had was at Diwali, but the spiderweb op-ed was too silly to put on paper. Nixing it, I started to draw a cow in my notebook. Maybe I could write about cows. But I had no opinion on them other than that I liked to draw them. Maybe I could write about puns. Only I wasn't the one with strong opinions on puns. Noah was. He seemed to know what to say about lots of things I didn't.

I glanced at the calendar in front of me. Aai would stick a Post-it note on it with big assignments that were due. The neon pink Post-it that said "Op-ed" was loose in one corner, probably because she had already moved it from November to December's page.

I pulled the little square off December, knowing it might as well move to January, since I had no idea what to write about tonight.

I made a little star under Aai's handwriting and wrote, "What do I care about?"

That was easy. My family, my friends, swimming, and

school. And fitting in. But I wasn't going to look like a total loser and write an op-ed about how I wished I fit in better. And I wasn't going to write an op-ed about what happened to my uncle, even though I did care about it. It seemed pretty weird to have to write an op-ed that said hurting someone was wrong. It seemed like that should have been common sense to everyone.

I made another star and wrote, "What do I want to say?"

That one wasn't so easy. I didn't know what I wanted to say. Politics and protests and important things didn't matter to me the way they did to Noah.

I moved on with another star, writing smaller to fit my question on the little space left on the Post-it: "What do I have a strong opinion about?"

I stared at the words. I tapped my pencil some more. Nothing. I had nothing. Maybe nothing mattered to me enough to voice my opinion on it.

I flipped the calendar page and moved the Post-it full of unanswered questions onto the snowy picture for January. I still had time to figure out what I had to say. For now, I was just going to enjoy the rest of this year.

chapter
TWENTY-FIVE

$\mathcal{O}$n election day, our last day of break, we got to my old elementary school bright and early in the morning. We walked past a garden of brightly colored, hand-painted kindness rocks by the doors with messages like "Be kind," "Love yourself," and "You belong" written on them.

I followed my parents inside, taking in a whiff of the smell that had surrounded me for five years when I was younger. It made me think of the school library, my favorite place to be, but it also reminded me of the fifth-grade boys teasing me when I first started. I turned the corner for the gym, where a short line of people waited near a sign that said POLLING PLACE.

An old woman with a cane was standing by it. She saw us

and smiled, talking loudly and slowly, as if we didn't under-stand English unless it was slowed down for us. "Did . . . you . . . register . . . to vote?" she asked, making a writing gesture to go along with "vote."

Aai nodded. "I have my voter registration card and my ID."

"Oh, fantastic." The old woman smiled, leaning on her cane. "You came prepared. Good for you," she said, as if she were talking to a little kid, before turning to the next person behind us and speaking normally to ask if he had registered to vote.

Mr. Giordano was standing a couple of people ahead, along with Noah and his parents. They were talking about something boring like the weather. Noah and I left the line and went to the gray folding chairs outside the school gym to wait for our parents.

"I got the latest issue of *Musings*," Noah said.

"You did?" I asked. "Did you bring it?"

Noah shook his head. "They didn't publish my article."

"Oh." I paused. "It's okay. You'll have a front-page op-ed soon in the school paper. That can go in the frame. It will look better anyway."

"I guess." Noah looked down at his hands. "It's been so

many months and I still haven't gotten a cover. Sometimes I think I never will."

"Of course you will," I said, but he still looked down. "I mean, *orca*-course you will?" I tried, remembering an animal pun from the book I got at Diwali.

The corner of Noah's lips started to move up in a small smile. "Not *punny*."

"First '*shrimp*ossible,' now this!" I smiled, trying to make him laugh. "Are you . . . are you into puns now?"

Noah elbowed me. "I'm into serious journalism. Like op-eds. Did you figure out what you want to write about?"

I shook my head. "Mine's not due until next semester. I have a few more weeks." I quickly lowered my voice as Mr. Giordano headed out of the gym and exited the school. "Let's hope I find something I feel strongly about before then."

chapter

TWENTY-SIX

The icy January wind was howling as it body slammed our drafty windows that night. I had wrapped myself in a thick blanket to stay warm as I sat at the kitchen table, my feet on the vent right next to the sliding-glass door. I enjoyed the heat as I sketched a blue cow with the watercolor pencils Noah had given me. The TV was on in the family room next to me, as my parents watched the election results come in.

"Wow, Genesee County's precincts have reported," Dad said from the family room, turning up the volume on the television. "Sharpe just barely got a win there."

Aai was in the kitchen, half paying attention, half squeezing some lime juice to soak ginger and raisins in for another ayurvedic recipe. This one didn't taste quite as good as the garlic, but I still liked it.

"Kent County's in. Macomb, Washtenaw, Shiawassee. . . . Look at these numbers. The polls were way off."

I watched Aai put the bottle in the fridge, biting my lip at the thought of the raisins tomorrow, when they would be saturated with the lemon juice and black salt.

"I don't believe this. Oakland County went to Winters," Dad said from the family room. "It was so close. How could the polls have gotten it so wrong?"

"You should shave," said Aai.

I turned to her, stunned. Had Aidy talked to her about shaving for swimming? But Aai wasn't looking at me or my legs. She was talking to Dad.

"That mustache. Get rid of it. Don't give anyone an excuse to hurt you."

"Listen to yourself. You're sounding as racist as the people you fear. Do you want me to pull my skin off too? Because I can't. We can't change who we are out of fear. What do I always tell Lekha?"

My belly turned with nerves. I hated when my parents fought. It made me feel uncomfortable. But something about this fight made me feel scared, too, and the chaotic voices on the TV, talking about the election, weren't helping. "Himmat karke badha kadam," I said softly.

"Right. That is how we live our life. Bravely. Because we're all in this together."

"Tell that to our neighbors," said Aai, sinking to the sofa as the words PREDICTED WINNER: ABIGAIL WINTERS flashed across the screen.

The news cut to an image of a hotel in Grand Rapids, where Winters's victory speech would take place. Her staffers and volunteers hugged her. Red, white, and blue confetti rained down on screen as a couple of tears rained down Aai's face. And the wintry wind outside seemed to join in, its mournful wail filling the dark world around us with an icy sadness.

TWENTY-SEVEN

*T*he next morning everything looked the same. There was still snow on the ground outside my window. There was still organic oatmeal for breakfast. But something felt off.

I watched Aai run her fingers across the little rosemary tree sitting on our kitchen counter, still displaying the mis-shapen candy-cane dough ornament and crooked pipe-cleaner reindeer ornament I had made as a little kid in school.

"There are Christmas decorations and lights on every lamppost in our neighborhood and downtown. There's a neighborhood holiday party to meet Santa, and Santa leads a parade downtown and turns on the Christmas lights there," said Aai softly. "Our homeowners association fees pay for that. Our tax money pays for that. We are happy to celebrate other religions. But the one year you asked the homeowners association to turn the lights on early for Diwali, they voted no. Why? Why do they look down on us?"

Dad looked at me as I finished my oatmeal. "Lekha, why don't you get your bag ready for school?"

"My bag's packed."

"You can't say 'they,'" Dad said to Aai, ignoring me. "Everyone is not against us. You can't think like this. Look at our next-door neighbors. The Wades are like family."

"And look at our next-door neighbor on the other side," muttered Aai.

"The world hasn't suddenly changed just because of an election yesterday."

"Sure it has. Now everyone can act like the people who attacked Ajay and Joginder. Because our new senator told them it was okay."

I began to drum my spoon on the edge of my bowl as I thought about what Aai said. Were we in danger?

Dad put a gentle hand on mine, steadying the spoon. "How about we all step out and get the paper and some fresh air? Maybe we can go on a nice winter morning walk before school?"

"What's the point?" asked Aai.

"Lekha is the point. Your health is the point. You cannot go further into your shell because of what happened to Ajay, or because of the election. You have to continue to live your life."

"Continue to live our life? You are living in some fantasy world. Look at who our senator is. That is how people really think in our town. In our state!" Aai's voice started to rise.

"I'll get the paper," I said, standing up, hoping to stop my parents' fight. "Then we have to get to school."

I grabbed my bag, threw my coat on, got into my boots, and stepped out onto the icy walkway. I hopped into the grass, deciding it wasn't worth seeing if there was black ice on the driveway for me to unintentionally skate on, and grabbed the paper at the curb. Through the thin pink plastic, I could see Winters's smiling face surrounded by the patriotic confetti. I glanced over at Noah's house, thinking he must have stayed up all night writing his piece on Winters, and turned to my house.

And then I froze.

It wasn't because of the ice on the walkway or the frost on the windows or the light sprinkling of snow on the grass.

On our white garage door, in dripping black paint, were the words "GO BACK TO YOUR COUNTRY."

TWENTY-EIGHT

$\mathcal{D}$ad, Aai, and the Wades stood before our garage door, where Noah and I had taken countless Halloween pictures, just staring at the words until Mrs. Wade's phone alarm went off.

"Sorry," she said, silencing it. "It's time for the kids to go to school." She put a hand on my mom's shoulder. "I'll drive them."

Aai nodded. "Thanks."

A van full of little kids going down the street to the elementary school slowed down as the driver tried to look at what we were all crowded around.

"We need to call the cops," said Noah's dad.

Aai shook her head. "No. I don't want to draw any

more attention to us and make more people angry."

I wanted to disappear inside my jacket hood as another car slowed down near our driveway before zooming off. We were becoming a spectacle.

"We can't live in fear," Dad started, before Aai shot the scariest look at him and he closed his mouth.

"Okay," said Mr. Wade. "Then we need to paint over this garbage. Because that's what it is. Garbage."

"You'll be late to work," said Aai softly. "I don't want Beverly giving you trouble because of this," she added, talking about her old boss.

"This is more important. And it won't take long."

Dad nodded. "The old paint is in the garage. I'll get it," he said, walking up to the door to enter the code on the keypad.

"And we need to go or you guys will be tardy," said Mrs. Wade.

"Wait!" said Noah, pulling out his cell phone. He took a bunch of pictures and e-mailed them to himself. "We need to document this. We need evidence."

But I was already walking away, heading toward the Wades' car. I didn't want a keepsake picture. I wanted to forget this had ever happened.

TWENTY-NINE

I tried to concentrate on school, but it was hard. Noah kept bringing up what happened, and I was running out of subjects to change the discussion to. It was on my mind too, no matter how much I wanted to pretend like it never happened. Every time a kid passed me in the hall, I worried if they had seen what was on my garage, or worse, worried if they had done it. Not that I would have the guts to ask anyone.

My bod-*Aai*-guard was back on the job again too. Aai was scanning all the kids during pickup, like she was trying to figure out which one of them wrote on our garage. I waved to Noah, who had Journalism Club after school, and ran to the car as fast as I could.

"Everything okay?" I huffed, clicking my seat belt.

Aai nodded. "Everything is going to be okay."

Aai took a turn, and I watched the leafless trees lining the road. Their bare branches looked like open arms, but it seemed more like they were trying to scare me than hug me.

"They found out who did it?" I tugged on my belt, readjusting it so it was no longer digging into my neck. "I thought you weren't going to tell the police."

Aai turned into our neighborhood. "I got this app. You buy your groceries online and they bring it to the curb. You never have to even enter the store."

I bit the inside of my cheek. What did this have to do with our garage? "That's the app you got mad at Dad about, remember?" I looked at the back of Aai's head. A few strands of hair were blowing around her ear, thanks to the heat vent. "They gave you someone's tuna by accident last year?" I added, over the garage door that was still unoiled and groaning like it was trying to tell the whole world about what had been done to it.

"This is how we're getting our groceries from now on, okay?" she said sharply, pulling into our garage. "I'm not going to give these people another chance to hurt us."

I opened the car door, eager to get away from my snapping mother.

"Lekha, wait!"

But I had already slammed the car door, grabbed the key from under the stack of plant pots, and turned the garage door handle.

A sharp beeping sound went off as soon as I opened the door.

"What is going on?" I asked over the noise, looking around the laundry room for the source.

"I installed a security system," Aai replied, punching the year she moved to America into a keypad in the tiny closet right next to the garage door.

"But we never even used to lock this door."

"*Your father* never even used to lock this door. I've been telling him for years it's not safe."

Aai led me on a tour of the other sensors she had installed, on our front door and sliding door, as if she were showing off some high-tech bank security system in the movies. I knew the security system was supposed to make us feel safe. But it just made me worry more, and made me wish we could find out who wrote those awful words on our garage so Aai would go from being super weird about stuff to just regular weird.

That nervous feeling was bugging me so much later the

next evening at swimming, my hands were shaking in the pool, and not just from the cold water. I stared at Aai in the stands, anxiously checking her phone for security system alerts or a message from Mama or Mami as she tapped her feet over and over again. Tap-tap-tap-tap-tap. Despite the sounds of kids splashing and talking to each other, every little sound Aai made seemed to boom in the room.

"You have to focus so we don't lose the next meet, Lekha," said Aidy from the next lane, snapping her black swimming cap around the sides of her head. Harper and Kendall, stretching poolside, looked at each other. I hadn't paid much attention to my teammates in PE. We were grouped separately for wretched volleyball, and I was too busy trying not to think about our garage door. But the looks being exchanged were unmistakable. They must have been talking about me since we lost the meet before break.

But what were they saying? We lost because I wasn't focused? I thought it was because I didn't shave. Isn't that what Aidy told me? That I was in America now and people in this country shaved when they were my age?

"Time me, Harper," Aidy said as she climbed out of the pool and took her position on the starting block.

Harper grabbed her cell phone from the bench and hit the stopwatch.

Aidy was off. But instead of the fly, she did the freestyle.

That was my stroke. She was trying to prove she was faster than me. Better than me. She was trying to show me how things should be done around here. I wanted to speak up. I wanted to tell her she was being mean. That this wasn't how teammates should treat each other. That we definitely didn't lose the meet just because I didn't shave. But I just sat there, quiet. Like a good School Lekha. Thinking a million things in my head but never having the courage to let them escape my lips.

As Aidy zoomed down her lane, I watched her black swim cap get smaller. I couldn't help but think of the hateful black letters. And then I suddenly felt cold. Did Aidy do it? Was she so mad at me for us losing the meet that she got dropped off near my house and spray-painted those ugly words on my garage?

Aidy tapped the wall next to me. "Well?"

"Thirty-three seconds," said Harper.

She was a couple of seconds off my best time. And that was with her aerodynamic shaved legs.

"Cool," said Aidy. "I'm still faster at fly. I was just checking to make sure."

Coach Turner neared us. "Let's go, girls. Break's over. I want you doing your stroke until you match your best times."

Aidy nodded, a fire in her eyes. "We've got less than two months until conference finals. We can do this." She turned to me. "You're our anchor. You have to do this."

I wordlessly snapped my goggles back on. Aidy didn't write on our garage. All she cared about was winning. And they couldn't win without me. I was the fastest anchor on the team.

But if Aidy didn't do it, who did? Who did that to my home, to the place where I was free to wear Indian clothes, and play Indian music, and eat Indian food without anyone belittling me with questions?

I put my head underwater, trying to drown out the tap-tap-tap sounds from my mother. But I could still hear them. Like a trembling heartbeat. My heartbeat.

Maybe Aai was right not to tell the police. To just be quiet about it all.

Maybe Aai was right to be so scared.

chapter

THIRTY

*E*ven though I didn't want to think about the garage graffiti anymore, I spent the weekend brainstorming lists of people who could have done it. One of Dad's patients, Mr. Giordano, Mrs. Finch, a stranger. . . . I was not any closer to narrowing down my suspect list when Monday arrived. But Monday meant Avantika was coming back, and I was excited for the distraction from solving this mystery.

I rushed into Mr. Crowe's class. Avantika and Noah were already there, looking at pictures of India on Avantika's phone. I butted in the middle and gave Avantika a huge hug.

"How was India?"

She grinned. "It was great. And hot. Way hotter than

December should be. My mom said I got too dark there from all that sun."

I shook my head as Noah swiped through the pictures, not wanting to have to get involved in a skin-color conversation. "She's wrong to make you, or anyone, feel bad about the color of your skin," I said.

"Anyway, what did I miss?" Avantika asked, taking her seat as Mr. Crowe entered the room with a stack of papers. Apparently, she was as good a subject changer as I was when it came to talking about skin color.

Noah opened his mouth to answer, but I quickly spoke over him. "Nothing interesting."

"Ladies and gentlemen," announced Mr. Crowe, "hot off the presses, this month's school paper! And congrats to Noah for getting a cover!"

I turned to Noah. "I knew your op-ed would get the cover!"

Noah shook his head. "It didn't. It's on the back page, after the band news." He flicked his pencil against his desk a few times as Mr. Crowe started passing the paper out. "It's something else."

I raised an eyebrow at Noah when Mr. Crowe dropped the paper on my desk.

"Really powerful stuff there, Mr. Wade," he said as he headed back to his desk. "Flip them over and start reading. You've got ten minutes before we talk book reports."

I flipped my paper over, feeling Noah's eyes on me. And then my stomach dropped. There, on the cover of the paper, was a picture of my garage door and the words "GO BACK TO YOUR COUNTRY" for all the world to see.

THIRTY-ONE

*H*ow could you do that?" I said as softly and calmly as I could to Noah as we walked out of English. My mouth was dry and my hands were cold. I felt like I was going to hurl every time I thought about how Noah had described to the entire school how someone had come to our house, on our property in the dark, and vandalized our door. It made me think about those words I wanted to forget. It made me feel different and all alone, like a hundred-times-worse version of School Lekha.

"People need to know that hate exists in our town," said Noah as Emma walked by, trying to be polite and not stare at us.

"I didn't want anyone to know about it. My mom didn't

want anyone to know!" I paused, thinking of how angry Aai would get if she knew the whole town knew what had tainted our house. Or how scared she would be. Would I never be allowed at another sleepover again thanks to Noah? Thanks to the one person on this planet who knew Home Lekha and School Lekha? Who knew every part of me and knew that I didn't want this to be public? And what if whoever did it saw the article and came back to our house to do more stuff to us? Worse stuff? Like what happened to Joginder Uncle and Ajay Mama? My throat felt like it was getting constricted as Noah's voice grew.

"I didn't say who it happened to, and the picture is a close-up of the garage. It's unrecognizable."

Avantika looked at the paper, confused. "Wait. This story is about you? This happened on our street?"

Harper glanced over at me as she passed us, eyebrows furrowed like she was solving a puzzle, as she kept looking between the paper in her hand and me.

"Shh," I hissed, hoping Harper wouldn't figure out the garage was my garage. "Yeah. It happened on our street. To my house. Do you have any clue how humiliating that is, Noah? I don't want everyone here talking about me."

"But I kept it anonymous!"

"There are like five kids in this whole school who aren't white! Everyone knows it's about me," I snapped as we neared Noah's history classroom.

"Someone had to do something. You weren't speaking up. It's like what I told you over break. Sometimes the person who is safe in the situation has to speak up. It's called being an ally—"

"I don't want you to speak up for me! You've never done it before. I'm pretty sure you just look down when Liam says stuff to me, so don't act like you were doing this because you always speak out against what's wrong. Or because I needed your help. Or because it wasn't safe for me, so you decided to do it for me. You just did this to get your front-page story! Well, congrats. You got it. So I hope you're happy now. Go shove it in your frame for everyone to see."

A few kids reading their papers by a KINDNESS IS KOOL sign looked at me as I stormed away from Noah's class, Avantika trying to keep up.

"He was only trying to help, Lekha. Be mad at whoever wrote that on your garage."

A group of eighth graders passed, looking me up and

down. More questions. They were wondering if the front-page story was about me. I just knew it. I couldn't take any more questioning looks, or quizzical faces, or inquiring minds. I didn't owe anyone any answers. I was drained from having to answer for who I was. I was tired of always being different. Of being less than. And who was Avantika to tell me who I should be mad at? She had no idea what it was like to grow up looking different from everyone. She grew up in a country full of Indians who spoke her language and ate her food and danced her dances and knew her movie stars. That's why she could stand up for herself that first day in class, and that's why she could stand up for me in the cafeteria. She could do it because she had no clue what it was like to be the kid everyone has questions about. I turned to her, my heart thumping in my chest as I thought about how unfair it all was.

"I'm not mad. For all we know, they meant to do it to your house."

"What?"

"Yeah," I said, louder than I had ever spoken in these halls before. "Like an Anju-Manju situation. I'm American. So what country could I possibly go back to? You're the one with the accent," I said, making sure the eighth graders heard, making sure they'd finally ask questions about someone else for once.

Avantika's eyes started to get shiny with tears, and I immediately regretted my words. "I'm sorry."

"It's okay."

"No, it's not. All this bad stuff has been happening, with my family and my team, and I didn't get to talk to you properly that morning you left after all that drama with the sleepover and swimming and shaving, and there's so much I have to tell you and—"

"We didn't have a sleepover when you last saw me."

"Yeah, no." My palms started to sweat at my slipup. "It was so long ago," I fumbled, trying to cover. "I meant . . . I meant, when I was with my team."

"Your team. . . . That's who was laughing when you canceled on me."

I felt my stomach drop. And the flushed look on Avantika's face was leaving me with a sickening feeling in my gut.

"That's where you were coming back from that morning. You had a sleepover with them instead of me." Avantika blinked away her tears. "I guess you got over that exhaustion pretty quickly."

I shook my head, searching for the right words to make this better. "I'm sorry."

Avantika shrugged. "I get it. They don't have accents to embarrass you. They were laughing at me, right? You all were?"

My ears felt like they were scorching hot as everyone in the hall stared our way. Was she really making this about her after everything I had been through? My uncle got attacked. My house was defaced. My team thought I was some loser who wasn't old enough or American enough to shave. I was the one getting all the looks in school, thanks to Noah.

"Maybe this really was meant for me," Avantika added, tossing the paper in the recycling bin nearby.

I squeezed the straps of my backpack tightly and felt my voice rise up my throat like venom. "Yeah. Maybe it really was." With the eyes of the whole school on me, I turned down the hall for science, leaving my friends far behind.

chapter

THIRTY-TWO

I spent the rest of the week avoiding Avantika and Noah at school. I found a spot on the far side of the cafeteria and would eat my meal quickly, and then stare at my homework in order to not make eye contact with my former friends or the people who were watching me sit by myself like a loser.

On the weekend Deepika Auntie came over with a shopping bag from India, made from folded newspapers. Avantika was not with her.

Auntie and Aai hugged, and Deepika Auntie began pulling stuff out of the bag, covering our kitchen table. She had brought us gulachi poli, stuffed with sweet jaggery and cardamom. She had packets of homemade aavalyachi supari, shredded gooseberry that had been salted and dried, a new Kalnirnay—the vertical calendar Aai kept in her room, and a black and gold shawl for Aai.

"You brought us so much!" exclaimed Aai.

"There's one more thing for Lekha in here," Auntie said, taking out a little orange plastic bag with handles. "You've been so good to us. Making us feel so safe in this new place."

A tear fell from Aai's face onto the newspaper crossword puzzle before her. "I don't know that we should feel safe here."

Deepika Auntie rushed to Aai's side. She looked at me and subtly pumped her palm at me with an "I've got this" gesture.

"I'll go to my room."

Auntie nodded. "Avantika and Noah are playing in the snow if you're interested in joining them."

I smiled respectfully and headed outside, feeling awful as I heard Aai sob into Deepika Auntie's shoulder as she told her what had happened while they were in India.

I stepped onto the porch, hugging my shoulders even though the cold hadn't hit me yet. I wasn't going to the backyard, though. I was going to get the mail. I walked down the driveway, making sure not to look back at that blank canvas of a garage door that made me feel ashamed and angry all at once. Making sure not to crane my neck to get a peek at my former friends in Noah's backyard.

I grabbed a handful of mail from the mailbox, squeaking its door shut. Avantika and Noah were being awfully quiet for people having fun outside. *I hope they aren't having any fun without me*, I thought as I rushed back inside.

I normally would have dropped the mail off in the kitchen, but I didn't want to have to explain to Auntie why I wasn't playing with Avantika outside. So I headed right up to my room. I could still hear Aai talking about Ajay Mama, Joginder Uncle, and the garage through the vent by my window. I neared it, feeling the warmth on my toes.

A bright sunbeam was on my yellow desk. I looked at the Post-it notes of assignments on the desk calendar and pulled my curtain back, filling the room with more light, shining on all my posters of Aamir Khan and the paintings of Ganpati and Lakshmi on my walls. It was happy and cheerful up here, totally the opposite of what I was feeling. And then I heard laughter. Squealing, joyful laughter.

They were having fun.

I glanced out the window. My backyard was a blank sheet

of snow with no sight of the faint rabbit tracks that were often there in the morning. But there was a slew of footprints on the border of our yard and Noah's. I craned my neck to see an entire snowman family. Noah and Avantika, wearing a newly crocheted orange fox hat, were in the midst of a full-blown snowball fight after building the snow people.

I slid the curtains shut, remembering how Aai used to say when I played with Noah in the backyard and she was out on a walk, my laughter was so loud, she could hear it drifting down the street.

Through the vent, I could hear echoes of Deepika Auntie talking about her cousin in Ohio who was told by a stranger at a grocery store to please go back to India after he got his degree because her daughter was having a hard time finding a job and didn't need more competition from foreigners. Then the conversation went back to the garage door scrawl Avantika had probably already told Auntie all about.

I had read enough about it in the paper, thanks to my traitor neighbor. I didn't need to hear any more, so I blew the dust off Dad's old CD player on my dresser and played a scratched-up CD from the black-and-white days of Hindi movies. The songs were slow and sad, a perfect way to cover up what Aai and Auntie were talking about downstairs.

I plopped down at my desk and turned its little lamp on. Aai had pinned my new schedule to the bulletin board above it. It had just come this week, and I couldn't wait for all new classes to start on Monday, for a chance to see Noah and Avantika even less. Or even more. We weren't talking when the schedule came, so I had no idea if we would have classes together. I reminded myself I didn't miss them. That I was mad at them, and glanced at the pink Post-it stuck to my calendar with "op-ed" circled on it.

I looked at all the unanswered questions below. The new semester meant I had only a few more weeks to answer them and turn my op-ed in on time. Like a good Desi kid.

I sifted through the mail, wondering if Mr. Crowe would accept an op-ed about bad friends. I put all the medical conference flyers in one pile for Dad. I put the junk mail in a pile for recycling. I put the grocery flyers in a pile for Aai, although I wasn't sure she needed them anymore with her new app. And I went to put this month's copy of the *International Indian News* at the top of Dad's pile, when I felt my insides fold over.

There, on the front page of the Indian American newspaper, was a cell phone image of Joginder Uncle in a hospital bed, his face swollen and blue. Next to it was a picture of Ajay Mama's face after the attack. It was the image my parents didn't want me to see.

I stared at Ajay Mama's familiar face in the picture. Only it wasn't his *familiar* face. His eye was bandaged up and he had big black bruises all around the socket. The white of the other eye was now all splotches of red from the burst blood vessels. And there was no sign of his beaming smile from the old picture in Aai's room.

I felt queasy as I stared at the article, titled "Will the Hate Ever Stop?" It talked about how many more reported hate crimes there were this year than last year against people of South Asian descent. It talked about a vandalized Jain temple. It talked about a Muslim uncle and auntie who were beaten up in their gas station. It talked about a Sikh uncle who was killed in his own driveway as he watered his flowers.

My hands got sweaty and I quickly got up to drop the paper and Dad's mail in the hall outside my room and shut my door. But moving the paper and those sickening pictures and facts out of sight didn't mean all these awful things weren't happening. This was what Noah was talking about.

This was what happened when hate went unchecked. When people heard hate being voiced and didn't stop it and let it fester and grow until it was used to hurt someone else.

I sank at my desk, thinking about all the people hurting. Thinking about what Aai would feel when she saw that newspaper and her brother's face. Thinking about all the little pieces of hate I heard every day at school, and the big piece of hate that had been scribbled on my house. Then the old CD got stuck, and I could once again hear Deepika Auntie through the register. She was asking a million questions. "Has this ever happened before? Isn't America safe? Why did we move here?"

All those questions made me think about the questions I thought I couldn't answer, the questions I was sick of hearing . . . the answers I wish I had the courage to give. I grabbed a pencil and started to write in my notebook. Fast. My hand cramped as I tried to keep up with the thoughts that were pouring out of me, unsure that I would still be able to just blend in after everyone at school read what I was writing. But it didn't matter. I had to do it.

No more changing the subject. It was time to address the subject.

I had to start speaking up.

THIRTY-THREE

The first half of my new schedule was Noah- and Avantika-free. It was also free of any more chances to stand up for myself. Liam and Mikey were not in my history, science, or math classes before lunch, and neither was Aidy. But my earlier relief was now giving way to nervous jitters as I settled into the solo spot I had been sitting at in the cafeteria since the fight. Liam and Mikey were definitely in this lunch period. And at least one of them would be saying something to me. I wasn't sure I'd be as brave as I was when I wrote my op-ed. But after what I wrote, I would be a hypocrite not to at least try to speak up once in a while.

I had just unzipped my lunch bag when Harper quickly sat next to me. I stared at her. Was this actually happening?

Was Harper going to eat lunch with me because I was all alone? I knew I could feel confident with Harper by my side. I'd feel strong. I'd be able to do anything.

"I have to get back to my table, but I just wanted to ask you to please, please, please think about what Aidy said about the razors."

I pulled my sandwich out. Of course she wasn't going to sit with me.

"She brings it up all the time. I can't take it anymore."

"We lost even though you guys shaved," I said softly.

"Yeah, but that was with three-fourths of us shaving. Just think about how much better we would do if we all did it. Just think about it before conference finals, please, Lekha?"

I frowned at her question, thinking about what I had written this weekend and how it had made me feel. "My name . . . my name is actually pronounced 'LAY-khaa,'" I blurted out, taking a long sip of my water bottle to avoid looking at Harper. Despite the cold steel bottle in my hands, I was sweating. I mean, sure, I had changed the subject from razors. But I had also spoken up for myself a little bit about something that had been bugging me for years, hadn't I?

"Isn't that what I said?" Harper asked, confusion wrinkled into her scrunched eyebrows.

I shook my head.

"Okay, Lekha," Harper said correctly, with a smile. "You think about the razors; I'll work on saying your name right, deal?"

I nodded as Harper got up as quickly as she sat down and headed for her table, just missing a collision with Liam, who decided he also needed to stop by my table. I took a deep breath as he smiled at me.

"Super-important question for you," he began.

I exhaled, feeling my wimpy breath shiver as I braced for whatever it was Liam was going to ask. I had to do this. I had to stop the questions, even if Harper wasn't by my side.

"Do you and Avantika ever sit next to each other and play connect the dots, Dot?"

I fiddled with my lunch bag strap as I ran comebacks through my head: *"That's not my name." "Don't call me that." "My name's Lekha." "I prefer color by number."* I settled on one and looked up, ready to let the new Lekha's voice be heard: "That . . ." I trailed off before I could even finish the first word. Liam was long gone.

My heart began to beat normally again as I told myself I was okay. It was okay. Sometimes big changes took little baby steps. I had told Harper the right way to say my name. It was a good-enough first attempt at standing up for myself.

I started to take a bite of my PBJ when I noticed a slight shadow over me. For someone who sat by herself, I sure was getting a lot of visitors today. I turned, expecting to see Liam again, or worse, Noah and Avantika. But it was Emma.

"Hey," she said. "Can I sit here?"

I scooted my meal over. I did not want to sit with Emma. No one sat with Emma.

She plopped down, scattering a bunch of pens and her notebook as she clumsily put her lunch bag down. "Look, I just want to say what they did to your garage is a load of crap. And trust me, I know crap," she added, showing me her latest drawing of pigeon poop.

I couldn't help but laugh. "How'd you know it was my garage?" I asked, hoping Noah could somehow hear her answer across the cafeteria to know his close-up picture wasn't as unrecognizable as he thought.

Emma shrugged, her forehead getting a little shiny as she looked around the cafeteria with an awkward, open mouth, as if she was too uncomfortable to tell me almost everyone in our school was white. "I just . . . I know Noah lives next door to you, and you guys stopped sitting with each other after it was in the paper."

I nodded.

"People aren't nice. So, I just ignore them. Sometimes it's easy, and sometimes . . . well, sometimes it stinks. But you just have to keep reminding yourself that what they say isn't true and it isn't right."

I smiled at Emma. "Thanks," I said softly, wondering if I was as awful to Emma as other people were to me.

I quickly glanced over at Noah and Avantika, who were laughing. I watched them squeeze grapes out of their skins like we used to do, and felt a little seed of sadness get planted in my belly. I changed the subject, fast. "You know, in India, I've seen cow-dung cakes drying on a wall."

"What? People eat them?" Emma looked more fascinated than repulsed.

I shook my head. "No. Not that kind of cake. Some people who don't live in apartments or bungalows use flattened cow dung to burn as fuel for the fire once it's dry." I watched Emma's eyes light up. It was the first time I could remember offering information about India to someone who wasn't asking me about it in a way that made me feel bad about myself. Or to someone who wasn't Noah. It felt nice. "I even have a pad of paper made out of elephant poop."

"You're lying."

"I swear. I don't know exactly how they do it. It's some old folk craft. They boil the poop for hours to disinfect it, and make it into paper somehow. My cousin bought it for me. A charity was selling it to raise money to help elephants in India."

"It sounds so cool there. I wish I could go to India," said Emma.

I smiled at her. We spent the rest of lunch showing each other our drawings and chattering away. As I got to know Emma, I scanned the cafeteria, watching my former friends, my teammates, and Liam. I turned back to Emma, cleared my throat, and started telling her all about the different birds in India. I sipped my water every now and then, but despite all the talking we were doing, my throat didn't hurt at all. It almost felt like my voice was growing stronger.

chapter
THIRTY-FOUR

*A*fter lunch Emma and I walked to Mr. Crowe's together for English. Avantika and Noah were sitting at the front, where we normally sat, but there wasn't an open seat near them. *I wouldn't sit there even if there was*, I reminded myself, heading past Harper to the middle of the room with Emma, to the two empty seats left.

Mr. Crowe began passing out copies of the book we had to read that month to learn about writing in verse. He stopped at my desk.

"I checked the portal last night. That is a very strong op-ed, Ms. Divekar."

"Thanks," I said, trying to force myself to make eye contact with Liam and the other kids who were staring at me, but I didn't really succeed. I did see Noah try to subtly eavesdrop by turning his head ever so slightly in my direction, though.

"There's a town hall in March that Senator Winters is speaking at. The same month your op-ed is going to run. Perhaps you should think about reading it there."

"I don't really want to say it out loud," I said, my throat suddenly feeling tight. Maybe I wasn't as strong as I thought I was at lunch. Maybe writing my thoughts down for everyone in school to see was a big-enough step for me. "Plus . . . my mom . . . I don't think she'd be able to handle that."

Noah quickly turned away from me. He was probably thinking about how he put the picture of our garage in the paper when Aai didn't want it public. I missed him, but I also hoped he felt bad about what he had done.

Mr. Crowe nodded. "Your call. I respect that. But if you change your mind . . ."

I nodded, cracking open the book and pretending like I was really into it so the conversation would stop.

I kept sneaking looks at Avantika and Noah, and every now and then caught them looking at me, too. I wasn't sure how long we were going to be fighting, but I sort of wished we were friends again. They had been having snowball fights ever since it finally started snowing again and I missed them. I thought they would enjoy Emma's company at lunch too.

When the bell rang, I said bye to Emma, who was going to PE, and headed for the door. Avantika was walking out at the same time, and we had an awkward moment when we both tried to exit at the same time and collided our backpacks.

"Sorry," I said, but Avantika was already through the door frame and turning the corner.

I took the turn myself, since it was the only way to get to my family and consumer sciences class. I was dreading this class. I didn't want to have to tell the teacher why I couldn't cook almost every dish we were supposed to make because I was vegetarian. Not to mention I did not have my parents' culinary skills. I burned my oatmeal at least once a week when it was my turn to make it.

I saw Avantika looking at me out of the corner of her eye as she left the carpeted halls of the English department and turned down the linoleum hall to FACS. It was also the way to the eighth-grade classes, I reminded myself, wondering if Avantika was off to one of her advanced classes.

But she turned right and entered the FACS room, and I had no choice but to follow her in.

Ms. Ross, the teacher, was standing at the front of the room in a bright-green apron that said HEAD CHEF. The room was divided into little kitchens, with two sets of tables in each kitchen for four kids to sit at. I headed to an empty table, but Ms. Ross called for me.

"Over here, Miss . . ."

"Lekha," I said.

"Leh-kaa," said Ms. Ross, butchering my name. Before I could even start to correct her, she pointed toward me, continuing. "You and your friend . . ."

"Avantika," I replied, since Avantika was purposely looking off into space as if she had no idea she was talking to her.

"Yes," said Ms. Ross, not even attempting to pronounce her name. "You two sit over here." She patted the table Aidy and Mikey were at.

"Great," muttered Avantika, and I frowned.

As the rest of the class trickled in and Ms. Ross assigned them their spots, she began going through the class syllabus before us.

"I'm going to introduce you to a new world cuisine or style of cooking each day, so that by March, you'll be ready for your midterm. It counts for fifty percent of your grade."

I turned the page to the midterm description. It said we had to make a dish that expressed us and write why on an index card, and it was due the same week as conference finals.

"Now, for today, we're going to learn how to bake a cake. Follow the instructions on the page before you. All four of you in your station will be making the cake together, so a team leader is going to have to assign the recipe tasks. So, get cooking!"

Aidy nodded, like she just assumed she was going to be in charge. Who was I kidding? With her personality, she always was. No one had the guts to challenge that.

"Okay, Lekha and Avantika, you guys can make the fondant so we can frost the cake tomorrow. Mikey and I will work on measuring the cake parts."

"Good idea," said Ms. Ross, hovering near us before leaving to helicopter-teach the next table.

"But . . . we can't eat fondant," I said hesitantly, hating that it was already starting.

"Why not?" asked Aidy.

"It's made with gelatin," I replied, remembering all the birthday parties I used to go to back when kids invited their entire class, where I had to skip the cake or Dad would cut the frosting off it when Aai wasn't there so that I could eat the part of the cake without gelatin.

"What's the matter with gelatin?" Aidy snapped.

"It's not vegetarian," Avantika and I replied at the same time. I looked at Avantika with a smile. "Good one, Anju."

But she didn't reply. I didn't even get a chance to see if she was going to, because Mikey started cracking up. "Wedgie-tarian?" he asked, mocking Avantika.

Avantika headed for the little kitchen, ignoring him.

"Why don't you try being nice for once?" I paused, stunned I had said something back so easily, without thinking about a million comebacks first. I guess my op-ed had changed me a little, even if I hadn't corrected the way Ms. Ross or the rest of the school said my name.

Aidy raised an eyebrow at me. "Okay, guys. Relax. How about Lekha and Avantika work on the cake, and Mikey and I make the fondant?"

I nodded, handing Avantika the bag of flour as she reached for a measuring cup, thinking she would be shocked

I said anything to Mikey, wishing she would tell me that it was so cool to see me being as brave as her, hoping she would have been happy I finally stood up for her after the way I had acted during our fight. But Avantika ignored me, grabbed the sugar, and began measuring that instead.

I put the bag down on the table with a powdery plop. Maybe this friendship really had reached its expiration date.

THIRTY-FIVE

I chewed on the sweet gulachi poli Deepika Auntie had brought us from India and tried not to think about Avantika as Dad worked on dictations in the Jungle and Aai got dressed all in black. It wasn't for a funeral. We wore white to funerals. It was for Sankrant, the midwinter festival celebrating the sun moving north, and the only festival based on the solar calendar instead of the lunar one, so it was always on the same date. Women wore black because it absorbed the sun's heat, went to haldi kunku parties, and got gifts from whoever was hosting.

When I was younger, we used to go to Tanvi's for Sankrant, and they used to give gifts to girls, too. Maya's brother and all the boys used to get mad about how sexist it was that we got gifts and they didn't. I wouldn't have to hear any complaints today, though, because the haldi kunku party was at Avantika's, and I wasn't going.

Aai called from upstairs. "Lekha, would you please find that shawl Auntie gave me? It will go perfectly with this."

Deciding to top off my sugar high with a grand finale, I snuck a bite of tilgul vadi, the rectangular-shaped jaggery and sesame seed sweets Aai had made for the party, got up, washed my hands, and headed to the bottom of the stairs. "Where is it?" I called back to her.

"There's a bag from India here," said Dad from the Jungle next door.

I entered the den as quietly as I could while Dad recorded his dictations into a headset. At the top of a growing pile of mail on a table was the bag from Deepika Auntie. I opened it and grabbed the black shawl. Under it was the orange plastic bag Auntie had said was for me. I had completely forgotten about it.

I slipped out of the room and crouched on the bottom of the stairs, opening my present. It was a sparkling magenta Anarkali with lime-green and orange chudidar leggings and an orange odhani. It was the most beautiful, fashionable outfit I had ever seen, and it was mine. There was a little card at the bottom of the bag. I opened it and read Avantika's flowing cursive.

"Knock-knock. Who's there? Aamti. Aamti who? Knock-knock. Who's there? Aamti. Aamti who? Knock-knock. Who's there? Varan. Varan who? Varan't you glad I didn't say aamti?" I smiled, continuing to read the note. "See? Marathi can be funny too. I thought of it on the plane."

I hugged my new outfit and ran up the stairs to give Aai the shawl, feeling like the worst friend in the world.

I heard some muffled shrieking out my window as I passed my room. I didn't have to look out the window to know Avantika and Noah were having another snowball fight. I turned and entered my parents' room.

The old wooden armoire was open, showing off dozens of brightly colored saris that Aai had folded inside. She was standing in front of the closet's full-length mirror slipping on a set of gold bangles, her black and gold mangalsutra, the sign of a married woman, sparkling on her neck. She bent down to fix the pleats of her black lace sari and pin them into place below her waist. Aai stuck a black bindi on and took the shawl from me.

"Thank you," she said, patting my head.

Aai hadn't really gone out since our garage had been vandalized. Even if it was just across the street, it was nice to see her dressed up and going somewhere.

"Deepika Auntie invited a bunch of the doctors from the clinic to this party. Think any of the Americans will be able to say 'Tilgul ghya ani goad bola'?"

I shook my head. That was the saying at Sankrant when you gave someone a tilgul vadi. It meant, "Eat the sweet and speak sweet words," and I knew none of the non-Desi people there would be able to say it.

"You're American too," I said quietly, putting the Anarkali down on the bed. I hated how Aai always called white people "American," like we were something different.

Aai frowned a little as she pinned the padar of her sari over her shoulder. "Isn't that outfit so beautiful? How thoughtful of Avantika. Auntie told me that because you weren't coming, Avantika went over to Noah's to play. Why don't you finish your homework up later and join them? You haven't played with either of them in so long."

I flopped back on the bed, deciding to give my tears a little help from gravity for their fall from my eyes by lying down. "Avantika never canceled that sleepover."

"What?"

"I lied. I canceled on her so I could have a sleepover with my swim team. After I missed the team dinner at Diwali, I didn't want to miss any more team bonding, any more inside jokes. Avantika found out and she was mad. Or sad. Or maybe both."

Aai nodded. "Lying is not okay. But I am glad you told me the truth today."

I fiddled with a sleeve of the Anarkali, sniffling as Aai sat down beside me. "I got into a big fight with Noah and Avantika. I was really mad at them and said some bad things. But now I'm sad and lonely, and I think maybe they are the ones who have a right to be mad at me."

Aai brushed my curls off my cheek. "I have an extra plate of tilgul by the stove. Maybe you should go over there with it."

"And say what? 'Tilgul ghya ani goad bola'? That's not going to solve anything."

"It's a good start," said Aai.

❧ ❧

As Aai headed across the street in winter boots and nothing but the sparkling shawl covering her lace sari, I trudged through the snow in my boots and puffy jacket, hoping my ski mittens had a grip good enough to not drop the slippery steel plate of tilgul. I didn't know if it was the slushy snow, perfect for snowballs, that was making this walk so difficult or if it was just the fact that I was nervous to talk to my friends again, if, that is, they still were my friends.

I made my way around Dad's garden, which was now in hibernation, passing the woody stalks of peony bushes, mock orange plants, and rose mallows that had flowers the size of my face in summer, until I got to the backyard. I could see the gray fin at the top of Noah's sharkphin hat behind the fort he had made. I watched as he hurled a snowball a few feet forward at Avantika, who was hiding behind the pine tree in Noah's yard. Noah peeked out of his fort grinning, trying to see if he'd hit his target, when he saw me instead. His smile disappeared.

"Hi," I said, my voice shaking as I gripped the plate as tightly as I could.

Avantika stepped out from behind the tree.

Somehow, talking to two people I knew better than anyone else at school seemed way harder than standing up to Liam. I walked toward them in what felt like slow motion, dragging out my agony, until I finally was next to Noah and Avantika. Their faces were no longer full of cheer. They looked frosty, like the snowman in the song, and their eyes looked hard and serious, like they were made out of coal.

"We have this holiday today," I said to Noah.

Noah nodded. "My mom's at Avantika's for it."

"Oh." I looked at the tilgul, glistening on the shiny plate. "Well, on this holiday, you're supposed to give people this thing I'm holding. It's sweet. And you say, 'Eat the sweet and say sweet things.'"

Avantika looked at me. I handed her the tray.

She took it, eating a vadi and offering the tray to Noah, who stuffed a bunch in his mouth.

"I don't have anything 'goad' to say," said Avantika after she swallowed her food.

That was okay. I did. "Knock-knock," I said.

Avantika and Noah looked at each other.

"Knock-knock," I tried again, glad my rabbit hat was covering my ears, which were probably red with embarrassment.

"Who's there?" asked Noah.

"Varan," I replied.

"That's not how it goes," said Avantika.

"Knock-knock," I said again.

"Who's there?" asked Noah.

"Varan."

Avantika shook her head. "That's wrong—"

"Knock-knock," I said, one last time.

"Who's there?" asked Avantika, her brows furrowed in what was either confusion or annoyance, or a little of both.

"Aamti," I replied.

"Aamti who?" asked Noah.

I looked down at my salt-stained boots. "Aamti worst."

Nobody said anything.

"It's supposed to be like, 'I'm the worst.'" I looked up slowly, but instead of seeing Noah or Avantika, I saw a snowball coming right at my face. The slush hit me and started to slide off in chunks. And when I finally saw Noah and Avantika, their eyes no longer looked like pieces of coal.

"I deserve that."

"Yeah. You do," said Avantika, a small smile crossing her face.

"I probably deserve one too," said Noah, flattening a handful of snow on his face. "I shouldn't have put that picture in the paper without telling you. But I swear, I was only trying to help."

I nodded. "It's okay. I'm sorry for saying you did it for the wrong reasons." I turned to Avantika. "And I'm sorry for being the worst friend ever to you. Manju would never have done this to Anju."

Another snowball hit me in the shoulder.

Avantika shrugged. "Varan't you glad I didn't hit you in the face?"

She ran down the yard, and Noah followed her. They ducked as I set the plate down, scooped up snow, packed it tight, and threw snowballs at my friends, my laughter finally at home, drifting across our yards like it used to.

chapter
THIRTY-SIX

$\mathcal{D}$espite the unusually warm winter, everything was finally back to normal in my world of swimming and school, even as the snowball fights started to turn into puddle-splashing competitions. Lunch and English class with Noah, Avantika, and Emma was always fun, even with Mr. Crowe sometimes trying a little too hard to be cool.

In FACS, Avantika quickly realized why working with bossy Aidy could be challenging, but we managed all right. While wondering what our midterm dishes would be (Avantika was going to make bhel because it had a blend of spices and was sour and sweet like her, she said), we even managed to make a decent stack of pancakes, baked crackers from scratch, and whipped up some delicious spaghetti sauce.

And in swimming, all the Dolphins were so good, winning our last two meets, Coach was positive we might be making State for the first time in a decade. I was finally back to swimming at my fastest, just like Harper. It was a good thing, too, with conference finals just a week away. In fact, I was so happy, I didn't even flinch when Aidy came up to me after our last practice and dropped a pink plastic razor in my duffel bag, begging me to shave before the big meet and not "ruin things this time."

I was ready to keep on having fun with my friends and keep on doing well at swimming and school as we got ready to celebrate the Marathi Hindu new year in Detroit. The Maharashtra Mandal rented out a high school for this year's Gudhi Padwa. The grown-ups were all going to watch a play from India in the auditorium while dozens of young kids hung out in the babysitting room and the middle schoolers and high schoolers hung out in the cafeteria, waiting for dinner.

Late, as usual, we parked near the back of the packed parking lot. I took in the muggy air, straightened out my magenta Anarkali from Avantika, and scanned the cars for hers, eager to see her inside. A couple of men were working on the large electronic high school sign by our car.

"Hi," smiled Dad, honking the car with a button to make sure it was locked.

One of the men gave a nod back to him.

Aai pulled her shawl around her sleeveless sari blouse. "You shouldn't be so friendly," she told Dad in Marathi. "Who knows how these people will act or what they'll do."

"'These people'?" asked Dad.

"Not everyone thinks the same of you as you do of them. Not everyone is happy to see an Indian driving a nice car around here. Not everyone is going to have a change of heart just because you say hi to them. Especially not back home in Oakridge." Aai lowered her voice, but I could still hear her. "I'm scared one day we will be driving home late at night and one of them will run us off the road."

I watched as Aai's nose started to turn red and she blinked back some tears.

"You spend too much time looking at websites about toxins and worrying about little things. Too much time hiding at home. It lets thoughts like these fester," Dad said as we finally reached the walkway to the school doors. "I saw you looking at that news article on Ajay and Joginder this afternoon. Why? It's been almost three months since that horrible day. They're both out of the hospital. Their breaks have healed. Their bruises are gone. Ajay's eye is back to normal. Why keep reliving the past?"

"You should have seen the comments people were writing underneath it. 'Good. Now the terrorists will think twice.' 'Go back to your sandbox.' 'Go back to your country.' Sound familiar? I'm not some naïve, paranoid person. This isn't the past. This is our present. This is our new reality. So instead of wasting time trying to speak to people who will never change, you should realize it's pointless and figure out how to keep quiet and stay safe."

"The world is still full of more good people than bad. You need to get out and socialize more. Maybe you should join the PTA."

Oh God, no. I briefly panicked, thinking of Aai embarrassing me as she tried to change the cafeteria menu to organic. As we entered the high school, the smell of ginger-spiced chai wafted around the halls.

"I'm here socializing, aren't I?" snapped Aai, her face twisting into a huge fake smile as she waved at Maya's mom and Deepika Auntie in front of the auditorium.

I said bye to my parents and ran down the hall to the

cafeteria, trying not to lose my chappal as they flopped against my heels with each stride I took.

Avantika was sitting with Maya and Tanvi at a table by the wall of windows on the cafeteria's edge. Tanvi was showing Maya something on her cell phone and snickering, while Avantika just stared out the window at the raindrops that were starting to sprinkle down on the school's courtyard.

"Oh, hey," said Maya, noticing me. "I love your Anarkali!"

"Thanks," I said, sitting down next to them and fixing my orange odhani around my neck. "Avantika got it for me from India."

"Aww, nice," said Tanvi. "Do you go back home often?"

"Her home's in Oakridge," I said, my bangles jingling against one another as I patted my curls over my forehead.

Tanvi rolled her eyes as lightning flashed outside and the rain grew heavier. "Fine. Do you go back to the motherland often? Is that acceptable?" she asked me.

We always called India the motherland while joking around. Of course it was acceptable.

"Do you really want to live here after living in India?" asked Maya quietly, seeming genuinely concerned. "Like stay here, I mean? I don't think I could do it. The shopping is so much better in India. The food is better. The weather is nice and warm. . . ."

"I miss my family. I miss being around my people. I miss the TV shows, the movie channels, Indian MTV, the Gujarati dance competitions, the Marathi singing competitions, getting to hear Hindi songs all the time on the radio. . . . But it's also too hot there sometimes. The traffic and pollution can be bad. It can be hard to find a good job with all the competition. I love India, but I'm starting to like it here, too."

"It's so weird," said Tanvi. "Everything you're saying is what our parents must have felt when they first came here, when they were fobs."

Tanvi's body jolted a few inches up as Maya not-so-subtly kicked her under the table.

"Sorry," she said to Avantika.

"It's okay," Avantika said. "How many years do you think it took before people stopped calling your parents fobs?"

"What?" asked Tanvi, totally confused.

"I was just wondering how many years I would need before I would pass the test and no longer be called that."

"Probably like ten years, maybe?" Tanvi shrugged,

totally oblivious to the fact that Avantika was trying to show her how rude she was being.

I fiddled with a loose sequin, watching as its metallic green color turned gold depending on how the light hit it, and felt sorry for Avantika. Here Aai was worrying about our present, with some people thinking we weren't as good as them. But Avantika would never be able to shake her past, which was just as good as any of ours, because people like Tanvi would always think she wasn't as good as them.

I pressed the sequin down flat, watching it all in silence. So much for speaking up. I thought I was different after writing my op-ed. But I suddenly felt like the old version of me. The old version of me who could have protected Avantika when Noah's story hit the front page but instead changed the subject, drawing everyone's attention *to* Avantika because I had wanted people to think it was her, to get a break from it all for once. And now, I should have helped again. I should have said something instead of sitting there voiceless, like the old version of me.

But it was like Aai said. Whether I was Home Lekha or School Lekha or Old Lekha or New, what was the point in trying to explain something to someone who wouldn't change?

chapter
THIRTY-SEVEN

*T*he rain was coming down hard as we drove home that night. The drops tapped on the car windows, sounding as loud as the time I had dropped a box of pasta shells and the noodles tumbled out onto the wooden floor. And before we were even halfway home, the sky began to groan and the water started coming down even harder, battering the car.

Dad had to slow way down on the exit off the freeway to Oakridge. The whole ramp was flooded with pools of water, and the storm sirens were howling.

"This should be snow," said Aai. "I can't believe how warm it is in March."

We turned onto the regular road, the winter potholes now home to rainwater, and the car hydroplaned, skidding across the water as the steering wheel spun out of Dad's hands.

"Careful!" shouted Aai as I clenched the handle above my window.

Dad regained control of the car just as an SUV coming in the opposite direction swerved toward us, moving out of the way at the last second.

He looked back through his rearview mirror. "I think they need help."

Aai shook her head. "They just tried to run us off the road. I told you this would happen."

But Dad turned the car around.

"What are you doing?" I cried. This could be the person who painted those words on our garage. Or it could be someone who saw my op-ed. What if Mr. Crowe showed it to a friend without knowing the friend hated people like us? Or what if the person who wrote on our garage somehow saw my op-ed and followed us, waiting for the perfect time to run us off the road?

My stomach dropped as Dad parked the car. The SUV was on the side of the desolate road, a DON'T LIKE IT? bumper sticker on its back window, its blinkers flashing in the downpour. My fingers felt clammy. This was it. This was the price of speaking up.

"It's a woman and two kids," Dad said, putting his jacket over his head as he got out of the car.

A few cold drops sprinkled on my face in the few seconds the door was open, and I breathed in the crisp, calming air.

"What is he doing? He's going to get us all killed," Aai muttered to herself.

But it was loud enough for me to hear, and I started to feel sick all over again. What if we were in danger? What if what happened to Ajay Mama and Joginder Uncle happened to Dad? Would we be the next article in that hate crime series in the *News*? I craned my neck for a better view as Dad talked to the driver and crouched down by the SUV's wheel.

Aai clicked her tongue and sighed. "They have a flat."

"What?"

"Their tire. They have a flat." Aai unbuckled her belt.

"Where are you going?" I put my hand on my buckle, but Aai stopped me.

"Stay put. You know your father knows nothing about cars." Aai opened the door and rushed to the SUV in front of us, rain pelting her expensive sari.

I gripped my seat belt hard, feeling the belt tighten

around my waist, trying to squeeze the worry out of myself like I was juicing an orange.

I saw the doors open as Aai neared. The driver and her two kids exited, stepping into the view of our headlights. And my hands went limp.

It was Harper and her little brother, Harrison. I quickly unbuckled my belt and ran out to their car.

"Are you okay?" I asked my teammate.

Harper nodded, holding her winter jacket over her and Harrison's heads. The rain was drenching my bare feet in my chappal, making them feel like they were soaking in the Sports Club pool.

Aai crouched in her sari and expertly removed the lug nuts. She raised the car up with the jack and put on the spare tire that Dad and Mrs. Walbourne had pulled out of her car.

Mrs. Walbourne bent down by Aai's side as she tightened the nuts on the spare.

"I can't thank you enough. The river on our side of town is totally flooded. There was water pouring into our house. I was trying to go to a motel, but with the storm and the flood causing everyone to evacuate, no local motels have room. I was about to get on the freeway to drive out farther when this happened." She began to cry. "Just when I thought things couldn't get any worse for us. . . ."

Aai stood up, the spare tire secured, the look of fear in her eyes replaced with a look of reassurance. "You don't need to worry. We're here. And we have room."

chapter THIRTY-EIGHT

The lights in our kitchen flickered as a flash of wintry lightning briefly lit up our yard. Mrs. Walbourne, Harper, and Harrison sat at our table, shivering from their damp hair, despite having changed into dry clothes. I sat by Harper, exchanging awkward glances as Mrs. Walbourne kept asking how she could help my parents and they kept telling her she was our guest and to just relax.

"I'm starving," said Harrison, swinging his legs at the table.

"I think you will like this Indian food once you try it," said Dad as he heated the leftover pan of paneer and pot of varan from lunch on the stove.

I put two wicker, peacock-shaped pot holders down on the table, and Dad brought the food over. He lifted the lids, and the aroma of lentils and garlic and mint from the paneer floated around us. Dad served varan in little steel bowls for everyone and spooned cubes of paneer onto all the plates. Harper scrunched her nose, trying not to show her repulsion.

Harrison was not as subtle, poking at his paneer. "It smells gross."

"Harrison!" said Mrs. Walbourne, looking at my parents. "I'm so sorry."

Dad smiled. "It's no problem. He's just a kid. Maybe we can make a sandwich for him?"

Aai dug through our fridge. It was loaded with vegetables and fruit, but there was just one broken end piece of bread left. Aai was planning on placing a grocery order with her app on Sunday, since we had been gone for dinner tonight at Gudhi Padwa. She emerged with a few glass storage containers full of pizza slices.

"How about some leftover pizza? I made it yesterday."

"Made it? You must be Supermom. When I want pizza, I just order takeout," laughed Mrs. Walbourne.

Aai smiled at her. I could tell she wanted to tell Mrs. Walbourne all about the dough conditioners in take-out pizza and the BPA in the grease sheet that lined the box, but she was stopping herself. I breathed a sigh of relief as she silently put the pizza slices on her iron tava.

Mrs. Walbourne stood up. "You can just—"

A crack of thunder silenced her.

"Sorry?" asked Aai, turning on the stove.

"You can just nuke it. It will be faster."

Aai took a second to answer, buying time as she flipped the pizza onto its face so the cheese began to sizzle on the tava. "Oh, that's okay. This is almost done."

Harper raised an eyebrow at me. "She doesn't like to microwave food," I whispered to her. "She doesn't like radiation."

I stopped short of telling her how Dad always tells Aai you get radiation just from walking on the planet, or that there is a lot more radiation when you fly on a plane, like we did every two years to India.

Mrs. Walbourne sat down as Aai served the pizza. "Gosh, you're really making me feel like a bad mom. You don't even microwave?"

"I don't like using radiation to cook food that my child is going to consume," said Aai, matter-of-factly.

But Mrs. Walbourne looked down. I could tell she was offended.

"Please eat. It's all organic. And the cheese is rBST free too."

Mrs. Walbourne looked at Aai as if she were speaking Marathi.

"The growth hormone? We only buy dairy without it. Actually, organic never has it in it—"

"Oh," said Mrs. Walbourne, her forehead getting shiny, like she wished this experience was over already.

I wished it was too. Didn't Aai realize not everyone was paranoid about stuff like she was? Or not everyone could afford the food she bought, which Dad said was way overpriced? It was almost better a few hours ago when Aai didn't think it was worth making an effort with people we didn't know. This was just embarrassing. Mrs. Walbourne must have been embarrassed too, because everyone was eating their pizza, which really wasn't as warm as it would have been in a microwave, and not talking. Everybody just went on chewing, pretending homemade pizza tasted good the next day and not more like soggy bread soaked with tomato sauce covered in cold, thick globs of cheese.

"To our dear old friend in the sky, good old pizza pie," said Dad, taking a bite of pizza between spoonfuls of varan.

"Is that a Hindi thing? Like a prayer?" asked Mrs. Walbourne, using the word for the language and not the religion.

"Mother!" said Harper, her face matching the cold marinara sauce on her pizza.

I guess both our moms could be equally embarrassing.

"No, it's that old song." And then Dad began to sing, and I began to slouch in my chair, wishing I could disappear. "My very educated mother just served us nine pizza pies."

Mrs. Walbourne looked at him blankly.

"You don't know it? My older cousin-brother had come here for his PhD in the 1970s."

"What's a cousin-brother?" asked Harrison, pushing his bowl of varan away.

"Shh!" said Harper, scooching the varan back.

"It's okay," said Dad. "It's another name for 'cousin' in America. His doctoral adviser's kids would sing that song whenever he would visit them. When he came back to India, he would sing it all the time. It's a way to memorize the planets. But now that Pluto, the pizza pie, is gone—"

There was another flash of lightning outside, and then all the lights in our house went out. Harrison screamed.

"Don't worry," said Dad as Harper consoled her brother. "Let me go start the generator."

I heard the noise of loose change and pens hitting each other in the drawer as Dad fumbled before finding a flashlight. He followed the beam of light to the front door and headed to the generator on the side of the house, which Aai had insisted we buy after a day without power during a summer storm years ago.

We sat in silence, chewing our cold pizza in the dark.

"This is actually pretty good!" exclaimed Harrison.

We heard the hum of the generator, and the lights suddenly turned on.

I looked at Harrison's hands. He was holding his slice of pizza, and it was coated in all the paneer from his plate and Harper's.

"It actually tastes better than candy on pizza," he said, chewing away with a big smile on his face.

I looked at my mom, Mrs. Walbourne, and then at Harper, and before we knew it, everyone at the table was laughing, together.

chapter
THIRTY-NINE

*B*y eight o'clock that evening, our house was full of even more laughter, and a lot more people. Avantika's family and Noah's family, including Cookie, were all in our house for the most epic sleepover our street had ever seen.

They didn't have generators, so my parents called them over. We made room in our kitchen fridge and in the one in the basement, which was mostly full of grains and lentils, for their gallons of milk, so they wouldn't rot in refrigerators that didn't have power. There wasn't room for the Popsicles from Noah's freezer, so Aai let us eat them all after checking that they were free from cochineal and carmine, the red dye made from crushed bugs.

Avantika's parents were a little uncomfortable with a

sleepover with girls and a boy, but not as much as Noah, who was forced to have his first sleepover. I let Harrison and Mrs. Walbourne sleep in my bed upstairs, while Noah, Harper, Avantika, and I set up colorful sleeping bags, lush brown blankets, and mismatching pillows in the family room. I got to share my sleeping bag with Cookie, who was the best foot warmer ever. Even better than the kitchen vent.

"I don't know why you can't stand her sleeping in your bed," I told Noah. "It's so cozy."

"Wait till your foot falls asleep," said Noah, rolling his eyes as he put on his noise-canceling headphones. He started reading one of my parents' old, sexist *Betty and Veronica* Archie comics, which Aai had agreed to give to me as long as I promised to understand they were from a different time, when some people treated girls like they were not equals.

Harper flipped through an Amar Chitra Katha telling the stories of the emperor Akbar and his witty adviser Birbal. I watched her face for any signs of laughter, but she was staring intently at every page, fascinated.

Next to Harper, Avantika started putting some lotion on her hands.

With no one looking at me, I took my big bun of hair out and started braiding it. I left the front of my hair pinned in place as I made eleven braids out of the rest of it. I opened the noisy lid of the glass coconut oil jar and scooped out a white glob, watching it melt to a clear liquid from the warmth of my hand. The strong scent of coconut filled the room. I ran my fingers down my smooth, heavy braids, thrilled I wouldn't have to spend an hour in the morning unknotting my hair.

"I heard the grown-ups talking about your mama and his friend," Avantika said, reaching for a dab of coconut oil. She took her seashell clip out and ran her fingers through her silky locks, which were shining even more than usual thanks to the oil. "If I had known earlier, I wouldn't have ignored you in FACS. I would have been there for you."

I nodded. "You're here for me now. And I'm here for you."

"Always." Avantika smiled as she dropped her clip into her bag and dug around in it, taking her Fair & Dainty cream out. She opened the lid and saw me staring at her.

"I thought that was going to stay in a drawer," I whispered, not wanting to draw attention to Avantika. There was no way Harper and Noah would be comfortable around a skin-lightening cream discussion.

Avantika snapped the lid open and shut over and over again. "It's silly, isn't it?"

I shrugged. "It's not silly to feel bad about yourself. I know what that's like. But you don't need to change the way you look. You're perfect the way you are."

Avantika squeezed the tube, leaving an impression of her fingers in the metallic material. "I'm not perfect."

"You're better than perfect. You're you. And I think I'm jealous."

Avantika smiled sheepishly. "That's not true."

"It is. You're confident. You speak up for yourself. . . . Why can't you do it about this little tube of cream?"

Avantika looked at me, and finally handed me her Fair & Dainty. "Okay. Chuck it."

"What are you going to tell your mom?" I asked, getting up to toss out the racist cream.

Avantika shook her head. "I'm just going to tell her I threw it out because I'm not going to use it anymore."

We shared a look, and then I went into the kitchen to throw the Fair & Dainty out for good. As I headed back to the family room, Mrs. Walbourne came down to the kitchen and Vikram Uncle handed her a cup of tea.

"Harrison's asleep," she said, inhaling the aroma of lemongrass and ginger. "Do you mind if we turn on the radio? I just wanted to hear if there was an update about our house."

Dad nodded, turning the radio on to the station it was always set on, except for Saturday mornings when my parents would listen to the Hindi music programs from Detroit. The local newscaster began talking:

"Many are wondering how much Senator Winters will do for the refugee center after its leadership accused her of running a campaign based on xenophobia and nationalism, blaming immigrants for everything from the loss of jobs in the auto industry to—"

Dad quickly talked over the radio while Mrs. Walbourne focused on her tea as if it were the most interesting thing she had ever seen.

"You girls ready for conference finals?" asked Dad loudly.

"I think so," said Harper from her sleeping bag. She twisted her body so she could see Dad in the kitchen. "Can I ask you a question, Mr. Divekar?"

"Sure."

Mrs. Walbourne put down her cup of tea and leaned forward in her chair. I wondered if she thought Harper was going to say something about Senator Winters. I wondered if the question was going to be another one that made me feel bad about myself.

"What is that thing you say to Lekha before we swim?"

Dad turned the radio down. "'Himmat karke badha kadam.' It's part of a saying. 'Himmat karke badha kadam, tere saath chalega har aadam.' It means to bravely take that first step forward, and everyone will be right by your side, because we're all in this together."

I paused, soaking in Dad's answer, and realized Harper's question hadn't made me feel bad at all.

"Wow," said Mrs. Walbourne. "Wish I had heard that when they cut back my hours at the plant."

"I am so sorry to hear about your job," Dad said to Mrs. Walbourne.

"Thanks," she said with a small smile. "That saying's really beautiful."

Dad nodded. "My roommate, Yousuf, in medical college in India taught it to me. It was when I started my surgery rotation and I had to observe in the operating room. It was a leg surgery. Nothing too complicated. But I wasn't ready to see all that blood. I wasn't sure I'd be able to stay on my feet and not pass out in front of everyone. I was so nervous the night before, I couldn't eat. That's when he told me this. It's what his mother used to tell him when he was nervous to go to school as a kid. It's what *her* father used to tell her when she was a kid, nervous to participate in protests against the British for India's independence."

"Amazing," said Deepika Auntie.

"That's really neat," said Harper.

"I survived the surgery, thanks to my roommate. And then . . . then I became a radiologist so I'd never have to see another operation again!" Dad grinned as the adults laughed.

I settled into my sleeping bag as my friends pulled their blankets up and began to close their eyes. No one was making anyone feel bad about themselves or wonder if they belonged. No one was asking anyone to do something they didn't want to do. Everyone was just together, side by side, getting through the storm. I cuddled up next to Cookie, the warmth spreading across my body, and shut my eyes, a smile on my face as I drifted off to sleep.

chapter FORTY

$\mathcal{T}$he air smelled like a strange mixture of crisp winter air mixed with a hint of earthy spring rain that morning. Power had been restored, and the Walbournes had left early, after thanking my parents a billion times, to meet their insurance guy and start cleaning up after the flood. With the electricity working, Noah's parents and Avantika's parents had gone home to deal with the spoiled contents of their fridges while we played outside.

We were using some of the hundreds of twigs that had blown across our yard in the storm to pick up earthworms that were in the process of freezing on the driveway and move them to safety in the soil.

"Once my mom teaches me how to make bhel for our

midterm, you guys should come over. I bet I'll be able to make it any time we hang out," said Avantika.

I struggled with a stubborn worm that kept slipping off the wet twig I was using, falling into a coil on the concrete. "I still don't know what to do. What food describes me? I bet half the school would think if you carved a jack-o'-lantern and then put a blueberry bindi on it, that would describe me perfectly."

"I think you're the only one who thinks that," said Avantika.

I gave up on the worm, watching it try to scooch away slowly, pathetically. "A lot of people think only one thing about me. You don't know. You haven't grown up with them."

"That may be true, but you have to think more of yourself," said Avantika, dropping two worms off in the soil below Dad's rhododendron.

"Maybe you're right." I decided I couldn't let the worm die. I took the stem of a stray maple leaf to boost the worm onto my twig and hold it in place as I gently let it go in the peony bed to the side of the garage. I looked at the spot where Dad took our Halloween pictures, at the spot where the words of hate once stood, and turned to Noah.

"I always used to think I have a version of me at home, and a totally different version of me at school. But when I saw what was on our garage, I realized there's another version too. There's the outside version. The one that some people can hate just by looking at me, because of the color of my skin, even when they don't know me at all."

Noah bit his lip.

"Your article . . . it brought up all those thoughts that I don't like to think about. I think that's why I was so upset. Because you may know what it's like to get made fun of at school like me, but unlike me, you have no idea what it's like to be hated by total strangers just for being yourself."

Noah's light skin turned pink. "I'm so sorry. I didn't know. I never meant—"

"No." I shook my head. "It's okay. After writing my op-ed, I kind of get why you wanted to put the picture in the paper."

"You do?" he asked, standing up.

"Yeah. It was wrong not to check with me first. But you were right to stand up to hate, Noah. To speak out. I tried to do that, but . . . I wasn't so great at it. And you're right too, Avantika. Sometimes . . . sometimes I feel like my voice doesn't work. Like I let other people say whatever they want to me.

I wish I could stand up for myself all the time like you do."

"The town hall is next week," said Noah.

"What?"

"The town hall. I heard Mr. Crowe telling you to read your op-ed there." He paused. "It must be pretty good if he said that."

I looked closer at the garage, thinking of all the times I let people say stuff to me and for me and didn't speak up. And the very few times I did manage to stand up for myself. I told Harper how to say my name, but I couldn't speak fast enough to stop Liam's questions. I couldn't tell a teacher how to say my name right, but I could tell Mikey to leave Avantika alone. Why couldn't I just be brave all the time?

I knew why. Because it was hard. It was hard to speak out against things that were wrong. It was hard to speak up for things that were right. And it was hard enough to do it at school, let alone in a town hall full of grown-ups.

I ran my hand over the new coat of paint. From up close, you could see a little gray smudge clouding the garage door where the words once were. It was like a stain you couldn't get out. Maybe if I read my op-ed at the town hall, I could wash that stain away once and for all. Or, maybe, if I did use my voice there, I wouldn't be helpless anymore. Maybe I could finally really start going through my life bravely. Maybe it was time to take this step.

I turned to my friends. "I'll do it," I said, my voice loud and clear.

chapter
FORTY-ONE

*Y*ou will?" asked Mr. Crowe. "That's . . . that's great," he added, recovering from the shock that I would read my op-ed at the town hall.

I nodded as I took my seat in English class.

Mr. Crowe began putting the school paper down at everyone's desks as more kids piled in. "It will probably be a good test to see how you'll handle the spotlight tonight when your classmates see your op-ed right now."

I flipped the paper over.

"Congrats on the cover, Lekha."

I watched as Noah, Emma, Avantika, Harper, and everyone else stared at the front of the paper at what I had written. Liam was the only kid in class staring at the other parts of the paper when I turned his way, acting like nothing had happened. But when he thought I wasn't looking, I saw him reading my cover. I caught some people trying to subtly look up at me, probably stunned that quiet School Lekha had an opinion. That I actually had something to say after all these years of silently taking whatever was said to me.

When the bell rang, Harper walked with me and Avantika to FACS, even though her class was on the other end of the school.

"This is really brave of you, Lekha. I can't wait to show it to my mom."

"Your mom? Won't she . . . not like it?"

Harper shrugged. "She tossed her Winters magnet and bumper sticker out when we went back home after the flood to clean up."

Avantika's eyes widened. "She did?"

"Yup." Harper nodded. "She turned red and said they were water damaged when I asked her what she was doing. But they actually looked just fine. I think she just knew they belonged in the trash."

When school got out, I headed for the doors with Noah and Avantika by my side, giving hard stares back at any kid who dared to look my way, like an upgraded version of my bod-*Aai*-guard.

"Look at what happens when you speak up," Noah said, giving me a proud smile before glaring at an eighth grader who raised an eyebrow my way. "And you were right."

"About?"

"I don't speak up when Mikey or Liam makes fun of us. I . . . I'm going to start. I need to practice what I preach," he added, before turning to Liam, who was at his locker next to Emma's.

"Hey, Liam!"

Liam turned toward us and then looked around, confused. "Are you talking to me?"

"Yeah . . . yeah, I am." Noah's forehead began to glisten, and Avantika put a supportive hand on his shoulder. "I have something important to tell you. . . ."

Liam frowned. "What?"

"Um . . . Kindness is cool, Liam!" Noah pointed triumphantly at the purposely misspelled poster above the lockers.

I tried not to smile as Noah's face flushed. He walked faster, shrugging. "What? I was on the spot. I have better comebacks when I'm writing."

"It was perfect." I smiled as Emma slammed her locker shut and caught up to us.

"I finished reading it. Everything you said," she huffed, out of breath. "My parents won't let me go to the town hall with you guys tonight, but . . . here," she said, digging through her bag. "I made this for you in art." She handed me a painting of robin poop in the shape of a question mark. "It'll be like I'm there."

I smiled. I would miss Emma, but I was glad Avantika and Noah were coming to the old theater downtown for the town hall with their parents to support me.

⊚　⊚

I entered the theater lobby a little late with Aai and Dad. Mr. Crowe was waiting by the question table to sign me up as one of the people who wanted to talk to the senator, and then I entered the auditorium with my parents and found a seat near the back. There were several arguments between people in the audience, and I started to feel a little nervous, especially when an anti-Winters protestor behind me, who seemed to be looking for a fight, started arguing with the woman behind him about refugees.

I squeezed Aai's elbow as I thought about my mental list of suspects. Having my words in the school paper was a big deal. But speaking here, in front of all these grown-ups? Someone in this audience could have written those gutting words on my home. Or maybe no one here had done it. I would probably never know. But would I ever be able to really stop the fear from silencing me?

Aai put a hand over my fingers. "I'm so proud of you, beta," she said. "You're not a baby anymore. You keep telling me that, but I think—I know—you're correct. You're not a baby. You're a strong, smart kid."

I swallowed hard. "What if . . . what if whoever did that to our garage hears me speak and comes back to do something worse?"

Aai's face twisted with worry. I could practically see her imagining every horrible thing that could happen. But then she took a deep breath in and exhaled. "Those what-ifs are awful, aren't they?"

I picked at the upholstered armrest on the seat with

my other hand, playing with some loose threads.

"There are so many terrible what-ifs that pop into my head all the time. But if you just think about the bad what-ifs, you miss out on the good what-ifs. Like, 'What if Lekha changes the world?'"

I stopped tugging at the fabric and looked at Aai as she continued.

"You inspire me, Lekha. You know, right after I quit my job, I took some computer classes online while you were at school. To become a website designer. This week I decided to dust off my skills."

"You did?" I said, ignoring the argument behind me.

Aai nodded. "I even got my first job. . . . Fixing What's the Mattar?'s website."

"Really? What about all the radiation?"

Aai shrugged. "You have to live, right?"

"Does this mean I can get a cell phone like Noah?"

"We'll talk when you're in high school." Aai smiled. "If the circumstances are right."

The lights dimmed, and I took my hand off Aai's, trying to read the op-ed I had typed up in big letters in the Jungle for my speech.

Senator Winters took the stage dressed in a sky-blue pantsuit with a silky red, white, and blue scarf tied around her neck. She waved to the crowd. When some people began to boo, others began to cheer loudly, while others started chanting, "Don't like it? Leave!"

The senator stood at a podium on the stage. "My fellow Americans, I am so glad to be here today, in my first town hall as your senator. I listened to you throughout my campaign, and I will continue to listen to you throughout my term in DC. So, without further delay, let's get to your questions and concerns."

First up was an old man. He told the senator he voted for her but had never voted for her party before. He worked at a manufacturing plant, and his daughter now worked there too. He wanted to know what Winters planned on doing to stop the big three American car companies from building more plants in Mexico and Canada.

As Senator Winters responded, a man patted me on the shoulder and said I was next. Aai squeezed my hand as I stood up. When Winters was done talking, and some people in the crowd applauded while others shouted angrily at her, the man turned on a microphone and handed it to me.

My voice was shaking as I spoke with my lips too close to the microphone. "My name is Lekha Divekar."

Screeching feedback made most of the people around me cringe. I quickly moved the microphone a few inches away.

"Hello, honey. What can I do for you?"

I stared at her. I didn't like her calling me "honey" like she was a sweet old grandmother, when the stuff she said helped people think such nasty thoughts and do such horrible things.

"Do you have something to say to me?"

I found Noah and Avantika in the audience. Noah had his cell phone aimed at me, shooting a video.

"Or a question?" continued the senator.

I reminded myself I didn't need Noah or Avantika or anyone else to speak for me. I could do this. I nodded at Senator Winters, steadying my hand as I looked at the typed page before me.

"Questions, questions, questions. I am so sick of questions," I said quickly, my palms sweating.

Noah gestured with his hands for me to slow down. I took a deep breath and slowed my pace, reminding myself how light I'd felt when I stood up to Aidy about shaving. Reminding myself how I needed the weight of all this hate to be lifted.

"Where's your dot? Where are you from? But where are you *really* from? Do you speak Indian? Do you speak 'Hindu'? Where's your accent? How long have you lived here? Do all Indians know each other? Are you 'Hindi'? Do you worship cows? If I showed you a cow, would you start bowing to it? Do you shower? Why does your food smell so funny?

"I am sick of being made to feel different. Like I'm not important. Like I don't matter. Like I'm less than everyone else around me. Like I'm not good enough. Like I'm not American enough. Like I'm just an unwelcome guest here that everyone else is putting up with until I leave." My throat started to feel funny and I blinked a bunch of times to stop myself from crying as I continued.

"I am not the enemy. I am no less human than my fellow classmates. I am no less human than anyone in this room. I am not something getting in the way of what you want. We all want the same thing. Why is that so hard to understand?

"On some level, I get it. The thing is, I did the same thing to someone else. I made her feel like she was less than me. Less American. Less welcome here. But it's wrong. I was wrong," I said, looking at Avantika.

"And what you're doing is wrong, Senator Winters.

Really wrong. What you're doing is dangerous. What you're doing hurts. Because what you're doing makes the questions louder. They make the people asking them stronger. They make the divide greater. They make empathy harder. They make compassion disappear. They're ruining our country.

"Yes, *our* country. Because it's mine as much as it is yours. I'm not a guest here. This is my home. I have as much of a say here as you. I matter as much as you. Don't like it?" I swallowed hard, wetting my dry throat, making sure my voice would be heard. "Too bad. I'm not leaving."

I clicked off the microphone, handed it to the man, and quickly sat down, my chest trembling. Mr. Wade whistled loudly as half the audience applauded and the other half muttered to themselves. I was just glad no one yelled at me.

"Thank you for voicing your concerns, young lady," Senator Winters said. "That's the great thing about this country. Everyone is entitled to an opinion. I'm afraid I'm not going to stray from mine. Our borders need to be secure. . . ."

I shook my head, thinking back to what Aai had said at Gudhi Padwa. Nothing I had said had made a difference to Winters or her supporters. Everyone had made up their mind.

"You were amazing," said Dad, patting my head as the senator finished and the next constituent talked.

"You're my hero," said Aai.

My heart was racing, and I felt hot all over as Senator Winters continued. "Do we have to stay for the whole thing?" I asked, feeling like I would cry if we stayed any longer.

Dad shook his head, and we headed up the aisle toward the lobby. I felt hundreds of eyes on me and people whispering as we passed. I couldn't tell if they were people who agreed with me or agreed with Senator Winters. After my speech, all the whispering sounded bad.

But I tried not to let it bother me as we entered the lobby. I had said my piece. I had done what I said I would do. I finally spoke back and spoke up in the biggest way I could.

"Young lady!" called a gruff voice from behind as we neared the doors to the parking lot.

I turned. Mr. Giordano was there. My stomach sank. I was not prepared to be yelled at by my neighbor. "Good speech. That took guts, young lady."

I glanced at my parents, shocked, and then looked back at my neighbor. "Thanks."

Mr. Giordano nodded, turning to reenter the theater, but then quickly stopped, looking back at me.

"My grandfather came here from Sicily in 1904. Everyone in town treated him like he was garbage. But he still fought for his country in World War I." Mr. Giordano's gray eyes started to be obstructed by tears as he looked off into the distance and nodded to himself over and over and over. "Yes. Good speech. That was a good speech."

I couldn't believe it. Maybe I couldn't change the senator's mind. Maybe I couldn't change most of her supporters' minds. But maybe I could change a couple of people's minds. And they could change a couple of more people's minds. And things could get better. Maybe, maybe, maybe.

I watched as Mr. Giordano waved to my parents and walked away from the theater, out the doors to the parking lot. Maybe he had finally had enough.

chapter

FORTY-TWO

*T*he week after saying what I needed to say at the town hall, I knew just what my midterm dish was going to be for FACS. It definitely wasn't a jack-o'-lantern with a blueberry bindi. And that wasn't just because Aai ditched her app and went in person to every grocery store in town, all of whose managers confirmed that pumpkins were way out of season. It was because I had the perfect idea for what represented me.

So I spent the afternoon mixing the dough and shredding the cheese with Aai, and the evening boiling and curdling the milk into cheese.

And the next morning, hours before conference finals, I dropped my dish off in the FACS fridge. After lunch, after Matty presented a soft chocolate chip cookie to show he was really soft and sweet on the inside, after Aidy showed everyone an old Polish dish her grandmother had shown her how to make, and after Avantika talked about her bhel, I was up.

I removed the foil to reveal a homemade cheese pizza covered in cubes of paneer, just like Harrison had eaten. It was paneer pizza, aka paneer pizza pie, also known as paneer pie. Because like Dad once said many months ago, I was as American as paneer pie.

That evening at conference finals, fueled by a bellyful of A-grade-worthy paneer pie, I sat on the bench next to my team, ready to swim my best freestyle ever. I adjusted my cap over my birthmark, briefly thinking about what I'd told Avantika about how it was ridiculous to try to change your skin, as Noah snapped a few pictures of me.

My parents, Avantika, and Emma were in the stands behind me. The Porpoises were next to us, followed by the Edison Electric Eels, dressed all in shiny silver, the Sharks, the Rockets, and the Dragons.

Aidy gasped when I took off my sweats to stretch and she saw my legs. "You didn't shave!"

I shook my head, a few neck hairs snapping from the cap. I was done with Aidy's voice being the only one we heard.

"And I'm not going to until my parents are fine with it. You're just going to have to accept that." I paused. I liked the sound of my voice when I spoke up. "Besides, we're still going to kick some butt. Because we are that good."

"Unbelievable," grumbled Aidy.

I stared at the rippling water before me. Unlike at the sleepover, there was no sinking feeling from Aidy's words this time. Nope. I felt like I was floating.

"What's unbelievable is you. Teammates stick together. That doesn't mean everyone does whatever you say. It means we have an equal say. It means we help each other. If you don't believe that, I'm not swimming with you."

"No!" Aidy shook her head. "No. You can't quit. We need you."

"We need each other," I said, my voice unwavering. "So let's win this. Together."

Aidy nodded, picking at her cuticles. "Together," she mumbled.

With the Aidy anchor no longer pulling me down, I turned back to Aai and Dad in the bleachers. Dad mouthed "Himmat karke" to me from the stands with an embarrassingly over-the-top thumbs-up. I mouthed "Badha kadam" back.

The whistle sounded for all the teams to take their lanes. Coach Turner huddled with us next to ours.

"All right, swimmers. You've got this. First place moves on to State. And you have it in you to do that. So, breathe, fight hard, give it your all. Do that, and I know we'll be in Lansing next month."

"Dolphins on three?" asked Kendall.

"Wait," said Harper. She looked at me. "Himmat . . . karke," she said, pronouncing it the best she could.

"What?" I was shocked.

"Himmat karke," she said again, looking at Coach, Aidy, and Kendall. "It means, 'Be brave.'"

"Badha kadam," I replied. "It means, 'Go for it. Because we're all in this together.'"

Aidy nodded, and we all shouted, "Dolphins!"

Kendall, Aidy, and I backed up a little as Harper got into position. When the whistle blew, she kicked as hard as she could. She was ahead of everyone but the swimmer from Preston, who was a couple of feet ahead. I saw Harper squeeze her eyes shut and churn her arms fast, so fast that she was now within inches of reaching the swimmer from Preston.

The Preston swimmer tapped the wall near us and then

Harper did the same. Kendall dove in, her legs wiggling underwater like a tadpole's tail until she came up for a powerful breath and started whipping her arms forward in the breaststroke.

I clapped my hands. "Let's go, Kenny!"

Kendall was on a roll, swimming faster than we had ever seen her do before, like a speedboat, pushing through the foam so fast, she overtook the Preston swimmer.

"Yes!" shouted Coach, pumping his hands into the air.

Kendall tapped the wall near us and Aidy dove in, her body cutting into the sheet of water. I snapped my goggles over my swim cap, ignoring how tight and uncomfortable the hat was on my big hair, and on my birthmark. I watched Aidy do the arm-burning butterfly, over and over.

But she wasn't going as fast as she normally did. The swimmer from Preston easily went past her. And next to them, the Eels' swimmer overtook Aidy too, followed by the Dragons'. My hands began to feel weak and clammy. How could this happen? Our strongest swimmer was suddenly our weakest. And worse, we weren't going to medal, let alone make it to State.

"You can do this, Aidy!" I yelled, my desperate pleas echoing in the humid room.

"Come on, Aid!" said Harper.

Aidy started to gain speed as the Preston swimmer neared our side of the pool.

"Push through!" screamed Coach Turner.

The next swimmer from Preston dove in for the freestyle, followed by the Dragons' swimmer. Aidy and the swimmer from the Eels tapped the wall at the exact same time, and I leapt in as fast as I could.

I ignored the shock of the cold water. This was it. It was all on me. If I couldn't overtake the Eels, we'd be in fourth place.

I turned my head to the side, arms smashing forward through the pool. I could see the bubbles being kicked up ahead by the Preston swimmer. I was neck and neck with the Dragons'. But where was the swimmer from the Eels?

I inhaled and kicked as hard as I could. The swimmer from the Eels was still making her way to the far end. I had overtaken her! We were going to medal. Now it was just a matter of finding out if we were going to State or not.

I churned my arms, faster and faster, my legs aching, my arms burning, willing myself not to look in the other lanes. This wasn't about the other swimmers. This wasn't about the other teams. This was about my team. And this was about pride. We couldn't lose in our own pool. I knew I could do this. The end was in sight. I kicked with all my strength for an extra burst of speed and smacked the wall.

The buzzer sounded loudly. I pulled my goggles off and stared at the scoreboard as Aidy, Harper, and Kendall crouched near me, poolside. The team names were all lit up, but our times weren't up yet. There was a problem with the scoreboard.

Slowly, the times started to pop up. The Eels were up first, several seconds behind even our slowest team time. Next came the Rockets and the Sharks. Then the names of the Dragons, Porpoises, and Dolphins. The Dragons' time popped on screen. They got 2:01.06. The audience applauded. So far, they were the fastest ones on the board. Next, the number next to our name came up: 1:56.39. The audience cheered as Aidy, Kendall, and Harper interlocked their arms. Coach stood near them, apprehensively staring at the broken board.

I looked into the stands at my parents jumping up and down in their spots. But we were still waiting on the technical difficulties to end.

After what felt like an eternity, the Preston time finally

flashed onto the screen: 1:56.20. They had beaten us by a fraction of a second. The Preston bench went wild, erupting into a celebration.

Coach clenched his fist at the near miss, but in a split second his expression changed to one of elation.

I reached over the ropes and gave the Porpoise next to me a congratulatory handshake before pulling myself out of the water. Coach patted me on the back.

"You beat your record, kiddo. Congrats."

I nodded, droplets of water making their way down my cheeks like tears of joy.

Harper and Kendall gave me a towel and a hug. Aidy sulked as the Porpoises shrieked and jumped near us. But I gave her a big hug.

"We got our fastest time ever. Ever! Just think how much faster we can be next year!"

Aidy looked at me.

"And we get a medal," I added. "A shiny silver medal." Desis couldn't be the only ones who liked shiny things.

"We should celebrate," Harper said.

"How about pizza at my house?" I asked. "We've got some cool toppings I think you'd like."

Aidy slowly nodded. "Okay . . . We really did go fast, didn't we?"

I nodded back as the officials called us over to the pedestal for the medal ceremony.

Aidy, Kendall, Harper, and I got on the second-place platform, just a little taller than the Dragons, and a little smaller than the first-place Porpoises.

I watched the Preston swimmers smile for Noah and the other photographers.

"I am so proud of you girls," said Coach as the officials neared us with the silver medals.

I glanced out at the audience, at Aai and Dad, who were clapping, huge, silly, beaming, proud grins on their faces.

The silver medal over my head, I pulled my swim cap off, letting my frizzy curls fall this way and that, off my forehead, revealing my bindi birthmark for all the cameras to see.

I smiled, my head up, bindi out. I didn't care who saw it. I was proud of myself too.

Paneer Pie Recipe

Be sure to ask for help from a trusted adult when preparing this recipe. Have fun!

Dad's Paneer

¼ cup fresh lemon juice or fresh lime juice

½ cup warm water

2 cups whole milk

oil for frying

Line a colander with a cheesecloth.

Add the lemon juice or lime juice to the water.

In a large, heavy-bottom pot, bring the milk to a gentle boil over medium heat. Stir frequently to prevent the milk from sticking to the pot.

Slowly add the lemon/lime juice and water mixture to the milk until it curdles. Stop adding the lemon/lime juice and water mixture once the milk curdles. (You may not use all of it.)

Lower the heat and cook for a couple of minutes and then strain the paneer (curds) using the colander.

Rinse the paneer in the cheesecloth under cold water to cool it down.

Wring the water out of the paneer with the cheesecloth.

Shape the cheese into little mounds.

Panfry on medium-low in 1–2 tablespoons of oil until golden.

Aai's Pizza Dough

(Adapted from Martha Stewart's Basic Pizza Dough Recipe)

1½ cups water

4½ teaspoons active dry yeast

1½ tablespoons sugar

1½ teaspoons salt

2½ cups whole-wheat flour

¼ cup spelt flour

1¼ cups all-purpose flour

3 tablespoons flaxseed meal

¼ cup extra-virgin olive oil

Heat the water on the stove on medium-low until it's warm. Turn the stove off and add sugar and yeast to the water. Wait for the yeast to proof (about five minutes). It will become a foamy mixture.

In a mixing bowl, mix the dry ingredients (the three flours, salt, and flaxseed meal).

Once your yeast is ready, add the yeast mixture to the dry ingredients, then mix the dough by hand. Slowly pour in the oil until the dough is formed.

Put a plate or pan lid over the bowl to cover it.

Let the dough rise for an hour.

Roll the dough out into two or more pizzas, depending on your pizza pans and your preference for thick or thin crust.

Oil baking sheets or pizza pans as needed.

Shred cheddar cheese, or the cheese of your choice, according to taste.

With your rolled-out dough on the pans, put your favorite spaghetti sauce on the dough and add the shredded cheese and toppings of your choice, including the paneer.

Bake at 420°F for 18 to 24 minutes, until done (the bottom and edges are brown and cheese is melted).

❦ ❦

Enjoy your very own paneer pie!

Acknowledgments

American as Paneer Pie is the book of my heart, and I'm so grateful to everyone who helped me create this story.

To my agent, Kathleen Rushall. I can't thank you enough for everything you've done for me and this book. It means the world to me, as does your appreciation for my Bollywood GIFs. I'm so thrilled to be on this journey with you.

To my editor, Jen Ung. I knew from the first time we talked how lucky I was to get to work with you. Thank you for shaping this book into what it is today. It's been an honor, and so much fun, to put this story out into the world with you.

To my parents, for double- and triple-checking my Marathi, my Hindi, and many of the cultural details. Thank you, also, Dad, for coming up with "Himmat karke badha kadam, tere saath chalega har aadam." And to the friends and family members who helped me with other parts of this book, including Gouri, Shaelyn, Supendeep, Neeru, Nirmal, Deepa, Geetha Auntie, Adil, and my mother-in-law. Any mistakes are my own.

To Brynn, Andrea, Dave, and Jim Burnstein.

To the kidlit community, including the 2017 Middle Grade Debuts, Team KRush, and the Renegades of Middle Grade. A huge thanks to Simran Jeet Singh, Tanaz Bhathena, and Ali Standish for your time and insight. And to all the readers, booksellers, educators, and librarians.

To the Aladdin team, including Mara Anastas, Chriscynethia Floyd, Fiona Simpson, Christina Pecorale, Lauren Hoffman, Nicole Russo, Caitlin Sweeny, Michelle Leo, Katherine Devendorf, Sara Berko, Laura Lyn DiSiena, Lynn Kavanaugh, Benjamin Holmes, and Abigail Dela Cruz. None of this would be possible without you. Thank you!

To Sachit, Apoorva, Baiju, Aashish, my in-laws, Cookie, Limca, and my friends and family around the world. Your support and encouragement mean everything to me, and I can't thank you enough. And, orca course, I otter thank my punny fronds Brynn, Casey, Kirk, and Eric for the finspiration for the puns.

To my kids, I'm so proud of you for standing up for what is right and speaking out when things are wrong. Thank you for striving to be kind and inclusive. I know you're going to make the world a better place. You already are.

Finally, to my parents. Thank you for everything you do for us. I am a proud daughter of immigrant parents, and this story is a love letter to you and all the aunties, uncles, and family friends I was lucky to grow up with—our American family.

TURN THE PAGE FOR A SNEAK PEEK AT

That Thing about Bollywood

*Y*ou know how in Bollywood movies, people sing and dance on mountaintops when they're in love? I wonder if they do the same when they're splitting up.

I walked my dinner plate to the kitchen sink, searching for the answer as I thought about all the Hindi movies I'd seen. The rules of classic Bollywood, from way back in the '80s and '90s, were pretty easy to remember: everything was loud, exaggerated, and colorful.

I scrubbed the miniscule remnants of green-bean shaak and daal bhaat off my stainless-steel plate. As the specks of spices, lentils, and rice slipped down the drain, I made a mental list of what you do when you're feeling a certain way in an old Hindi movie:

When you're happy, you sing, sometimes from a mountaintop.

When you're sad, you sing.

When you're really into what you're wearing, you sing. Seriously. There are songs about scarves, bindis, bangles, anklets . . . any accessory will do. I'll bet one day there will be a song about thermal underwear.

When you're mad, nope, you don't sing. But you can do an angry instrumental dance or scream while shaking in rage, and the soundtrack behind you will be full of *dishoom dishoom* as you beat up the bad guys and save the day.

And when you're jealous, you can sing or take part in a bonus dance-off.

Basically, anytime you are feeling something, you show it. So, I guess, yeah, you would sing in a Bollywood movie when you were breaking up.

I dried my hands and walked past the window with the swaying jacaranda trees in our backyard. I glanced at the white house behind ours with the clay tile roof crawling with purple bougainvillea vines, my friend Zara's house, and I headed into our family room. My grandparents' four pictures hung on the light-gray wall there with dried sandalwood garlands around them, symbolizing that they had passed away. Across from the pictures, Mom and my little brother, Ronak, were already snuggled under a blanket on our long gray sofa.

"What are we watching tonight, Sonali ben?" Ronak

asked, adding on the respectful Gujarati word for "big sister."

"Something funny," I replied, accidentally bumping into the stack of dusty books about the history of Hindi films on the end table. I straightened them out and opened the wooden armoire in the corner, which was covered in family pictures of us whale watching and at Sequoia National Park. I was extra careful not to knock over the new framed photo of my aunt Avni Foi, grinning with her fiancé, Baljeet Uncle, at their engagement party.

The armoire was stuffed to the max with old VHS tapes from when my grandfather owned Indian Video, a little store in Artesia that used to rent Hindi movie videotapes to people, before switching to DVDs. When Dada passed away last summer, he left all the store's retired videotapes to me, because he knew how much I used to love watching them with him when I was little. Luckily, Dada had passed his old VHS player down to me too, or I'd have no way to watch the tapes at home. And now every Sunday, my family got together and watched an old Bollywood movie together.

I wasn't sure how long this tradition was going to last, but I was going to enjoy it while I could. I moved the red, plastic, convertible-car-shaped VHS rewinder and grabbed a movie off the top shelf of the alphabetically sorted tapes. It was fun and silly, and from the lines in my mom's forehead, which seemed to be permanent these days, it looked like she could use the laughs.

I put the videotape into the rewinder so it wouldn't wear out the VHS player, popped it into the VHS player when it was back to the beginning of the movie, and settled in under the blanket next to Ronak as the ancient commercials that always played before these movies began. One was for a turmeric cream and featured a bride getting turmeric paste all over her legs before her wedding and a catchy song. Ronak sang along, tapping his toes. The next one was for a pain balm and also had a catchy song, of course, so Ronak kept singing. And then the censor certificate flashed, showing the movie's rating.

"Wait." Ronak reached for the remote in my hand and pressed pause. "What about Dad?"

"What about him?" I asked, swiping my silky black locks out of my eyes.

"We always wait for Dad."

I sighed. "And he always works and makes us wait forever."

Mom's fingers were clenched tightly around one another as she squeezed her hands in her lap like she was trying not to say something. "I block my whole evening schedule off at the hospital for this every week. But clearly he doesn't prioritize—"

Whoops. It seemed she didn't squeeze her hands hard enough and something slipped out. Ronak's eyebrows furrowed with worry, but Mom gave us a tiny smile with her chapped lips.

"Why don't we start the movie, and if Dad wants to see what he missed, after his client dinner, we can always rewind it for him?" she asked.

"But you always tell us to think about how we would feel in someone else's shoes, and I would feel sad if you started the movie without me," Ronak replied.

Ronak was sensitive and kind and not afraid to show the world how he felt. He would be a perfect fit in a Bollywood movie.

"Well, we don't wear shoes in the house," I said. "So don't pretend you're in anyone's shoes right now and just enjoy the movie."

I clicked play on the remote that Dada had always kept wrapped in plastic to keep clean. It may have saved the remote from sticky fingers, but it meant I had to press extra hard to make the buttons work.

"You have no feelings," Ronak muttered as the colorful titles began.

"You have too many feelings," I retorted.

"Shh," Mom said as the opening scene played. She smiled as Ronak giggled uncontrollably at Aamir Khan's antics.

I let out a puff of air through my nose at a particularly hilarious line. "That's funny."

Mom raised an eyebrow at me. "Is that your laugh? 'That's funny'?"

"Wouldn't want anyone to see your emotions or anything," Ronak said, before laughing loudly at the next line.

"Stop fighting, you two," Mom said gently, leaning into us.

I gave Ronak a small look out of the side of my eye. He was two years younger, but even at nine, he understood the irony of Mom telling us not to fight when she and Dad fought all the time. His eyes glistened, and I was afraid he was going to start crying.

I poked his arm. "This is the funniest part, remember?"

"Yeah." Ronak smiled, wiping his eyes. "You might even actually laugh out loud instead of just saying, 'That's funny.'"

But I didn't, even as Juhi Chawla made the most hysterical expressions at Aamir Khan on-screen. "That's funny." I said, and smiled with a small puff of air.

Ronak was holding his belly and laughing as loudly as Mom when we heard the garage door open, and Dad walked in, his briefcase full of papers from work.

"Hey, Rony-Pony and my little Soni," he said to us, setting his briefcase down and taking a seat on the other side of me without a word to Mom.

Mom suddenly stopped laughing, and those laugh lines that were on her face were outnumbered by the frown lines between her eyebrows as she stared hard at the screen.

I guess, unlike in Bollywood, in real life, people don't sing when they're growing apart. Nope. They're just silent.

$\mathcal{T}$he next morning, with the late-January air still heavy with mist, Zara and I waited at the top of my driveway, backpacks on, passing a basketball back and forth.

"Do you think if this acting thing doesn't work out for me, I could be a choreographer?" Zara asked, chasing after the ball as it bounced into the garage around my parents' white sedans.

My belly did a nervous twitch. It was not only the start of the new school week. It was the start of the new semester, which meant new electives. So Zara was about to get a lot of acting practice in, because today we started drama. "You're an awesome actress," I replied, skipping over how having to act in front of everyone made me want to hurl. "It will totally work out."

Zara gasped from the garage. "Oh my god. Whose are these?" She emerged with a dusty pair of roller skates with faded red wheels and teddy bears painted on the sides.

I grinned. "They're . . . my dad's."

"Your dad wore these? As an adult?" Zara slid her shoes off and slipped into the skates that were way too large for her. And then she immediately fell forward.

I dived and grabbed her arms, steadying her.

"That was so Suraj of you," Zara laughed, referencing the old Hindi movie hero who roller-skated to defeat the bad guy and save the day.

A cool breeze swirled past us, fluttering through my long black waves, and Zara flipped her own curly black hair like she was in a Hindi movie. *"Hawa ke saath saath,"* she sang. It was a line about going along with the wind from an old roller-skating song.

I glanced around us. Our street was empty.

"No one's looking. You know the rest." Zara put her hand to her ear. "I'm waiting."

"Ghata ke sang sang." I said the line about going along with the clouds, in monotone.

Zara dramatically kicked herself back, rolling toward the garage with her hands outstretched. *"O saathi chal!"* she sang loudly, telling me to go along with her.

Just then the door slammed and Dad and Ronak rushed

out. The gust from the door caused Dad's thinning hair to fly up off his bald spot.

"I think we have everything," Dad said, patting his hair down while glancing at his briefcase, a stack of papers, and Ronak's bag. "Come on, everyone. We're late!"

Zara bugged her eyes out at me, mouthing, "Busted," as she pointed to the skates.

I stifled my laughter, grabbed Zara's shoes off the driveway, and got into the car.

Dad opened the other door for Zara. She gave him a big goofy grin to distract him from his skates on her feet, and tumbled in. Dad was too busy reading a work email on his phone to notice, so Zara hurriedly kicked off the skates as I passed her shoes across Ronak.

"You're not going to be driving any clients around today, are you, Kirit Uncle?" Zara asked, pointing to the skates for me and Ronak to see as we all buckled up.

Ronak laughed, despite trying not to, as Dad said no and put his phone away. He then gave us a brief but boring overview of his day as he pulled out of the driveway and headed for Ocean-view Academy, which, despite its name, did not have a view of the ocean.

"Do you think Ms. Lin is going to have us sing and dance

in drama?" Zara asked, throwing the back of her hand to her forehead and making over-the-top Hindi movie faces as the two gold bangles from her last trip to Pakistan jingled against each other. "Bollywood-style?"

The reporter on the car radio began talking about a squirrel stuck in the tar pits, and Dad quickly switched to the LA traffic station.

"No way. There's no way she would do that." I sank in my seat. *Would she?*

"Why? We just had an awesome Bollywood performance," Zara said, making the roller skates dance out of Dad's view, trying to make me laugh.

"No matter what, Sonali, you have to do your best, right?" I saw Dad's eyes look my way in the rearview mirror. I bit the inside of my cheeks. I knew he was trying to remind me to get good grades this semester, after my last report card was less than stellar.

"Speaking of dance," Dad continued, "Avni Foi called this morning. She wants you and Ronak to do a dance at her sangeet with all your cousins, Sonali."

Zara squealed in excitement for me. A sangeet was an event before a wedding where everyone sings and dances. Her black curls caught the light from the window, turning a golden brown. "Oh, that's going to be so awesome!" She gasped. "You could totally do 'Dil Le Gayi Kudi Gujarat Di!' You know, since he's Punjabi . . ."

". . . and she's Gujarati," Ronak continued, as excited as Zara. "This is going to be so cool."

"Not really." I frowned, pressing down hard on the button to lower the window, letting in the sounds of the sparrows and warblers and traffic from outside. I always felt a little bit of motion sickness in cars, but this dancing-in-public talk made me feel even more nauseous than normal. I loved watching all the songs and dances in Hindi movies but felt ridiculous dancing to them in front of witnesses, grinning super cheesily at a romantic line or exaggerating my eyebrows at a sad one.

"You're as good a dancer as Parvati," Zara replied, talking about my super-talented cousin, who would be choreographing us just like she always did at family party performances. "You should totally practice when we're on the mountain for our field trip next week. Sridevi-style."

The thought of dancing on the little fire-scarred mountains over the 405 in front of everyone was mortifying, and a far cry from the snowcapped mountains or lush green mountains peppered with bright wildflowers that Hindi movie stars danced on. "You know I hate dancing in front of people," I replied as we waited forever at a red light on Wilshire. "And it's for sure going to be a medley at the sangeet. I'll bet Parvati will cram in, like, ten songs. My cheeks will hurt from smiling that long."

"Your cheeks can handle a ten-minute smile," Zara laughed.

"She's right, robot-sister." Ronak grinned just as the car speakers began to ring.

Dad pushed a button. Before he could say a word, Mom started talking, and I could hear her frown in every syllable.

"Tell me you remembered to pack Ronak's water bottle and didn't forget again?"

"Oh no." Dad groaned as he turned toward our school. "I have a morning meeting."

"Yeah. I know. So now I'll have to leave the hospital between patients, go home and get it, and take it to school. Because you can't be responsible and complete a simple job."

"Speakerphone on chhe." I saw Dad's ears turn red as he switched to Gujarati, letting Mom know she was on speakerphone. "Jara relax tha, okay? Mhari meeting bhaley chuki jaaye, hoon kari daish. Taari eklinij nokri bahu important chhe ne?"

Zara, who couldn't understand Gujarati but could definitely understand the tone being used, looked out the window, pretending the white-barked fig trees next to the sidewalk were the most fascinating things in the world. I looked at Ronak, who was staring at the cheerful teddy-bear roller skates on the floor as my dad told my mom he would miss his meeting and take care of it because she was the only one with an important job.

"Relax?" Mom snapped.

My ears burned, and I hoped the rest of my face wasn't as twisted as I felt. Why did Mom have to start this fight when she knew Zara would hear it? Didn't she realize how embarrassing this was?

"I'll call you later. I'm turning into the school," Dad replied, hanging up. He pulled to a stop in the drop-off line for middle school.

"Bye, Ro. Bye, Kirit Uncle," Zara said as she got out of the car. "Thanks for the ride."

"Of course," Dad replied warmly, even though I could tell he was still mad from the call by how red his cheeks remained.

"Bye," I said softly, following Zara as my dad headed down the road to take Ronak to the elementary school on the far end of campus.

"Smile," Zara said to me, linking elbows as she practically bounced. "New semester New beginnings. In just a few hours we will be in drama!"

I clearly had enough drama at home, so I wasn't sure why I had let Zara convince me to sign up for drama at school. But I took a breath and faked a smile as we entered the building, pretending, like always, that everything was going to be okay.

Maybe I would be good at this acting thing.

"Amina's anxieties are entirely relatable, but it's her sweet-hearted
nature that makes her such a winning protagonist."
—*Entertainment Weekly*

★"A universal story of self-acceptance and the acceptance of others."
—*School Library Journal*, starred review

★"Written as beautifully as Amina's voice surely is,
this compassionate, timely novel is highly recommended."
—*Booklist*, starred review

★"Amina's middle school woes and the universal themes running
through the book transcend culture, race, and religion."
—*Kirkus Reviews*, starred review